Both Feet In

Wildflower Valley Book 2
Kate Hewitt

Feathers Press

Feathers Press.

Cover design by Rachel Lilly and Charlotte Swartz.

Copyright 2025 © by Kate Hewitt

All rights reserved. No portion of this book may be reproduced in any form without written permission from the publisher or author, except as permitted by U.S. copyright law.

Chapter One

Predictably, we run into problems just five minutes after we arrive. I was expecting some kind of snag, but I'd hoped we'd have ten minutes, at least, maybe fifteen, before we began to seriously rethink this madcap plan.

Not that anyone was actually doing any rethinking. Yet. We'd just driven six hours from Princeton, New Jersey to Wildflower Valley, West Virginia, on something of a high, fueled by Starbucks ('last chance for a latte, guys!') and giddy excitement that we were finally *doing* this.

Six weeks ago, we decided, as a family, to pack in our suburban lives, both frantic and mundane, for homesteading in the country. It took my husband Josh over a year to convince me that this might be a not-so-terrible idea, as well as a few crises along the way that forced me to rethink my priorities as a mother, a wife, a *person*. Suburban life wasn't working for any of us anymore, with its myriad pressures and problems. All of us—Josh, me, our four children and even my dad—wanted something different. Something that involved chickens and tomato plants and maybe even a milk cow. So here we are.

Wildflower Valley is in central West Virginia, an area of serene mountain lakes and deeply wooded forests, with the rugged peaks of the Appalachians cutting into the horizon everywhere you turn.

It's thirty miles from the tiny town of Buckholt, having just four other residents—that we know of, anyway—nestled on the steep slopes that are named for the colorful flowers that, I hope, dot its meadows in the spring. In early March, however, the landscape is comprised entirely of stark, leafless trees stretching skeletal branches to a steel-gray sky, dead, brown grass... and mud.

Lots of mud, frozen into deep ruts but soft and sludgy in the middle, as we discover when driving through it, with Josh valiantly shifting into lower and lower gear as our minivan heaved and groaned in protest.

Our little house, subject to an imminent expansion, is perched halfway up one side of the valley, with its own tiny orchard, two semi-dilapidated barns and a chicken coop, and a sweet little pond fringed by birches out back. It's also at the top of a rutted dirt drive, several hundred yards long, winding its way up the steep hillside. Our minivan makes it up with some wheezy protest and a couple of clanks, but we are just climbing out of the car, stretching and trying not to shiver in the wintry weather, when the moving truck that followed us from Princeton pulls to a stop at the bottom of the hill.

"They're here!" Rose, my just-turned-seven-year-old, calls excitedly. My other children—Bethany, a semi-adulting eighteen, William, a studious fifteen, and Jack, an energetic eleven—all stop to silently watch the truck begin the arduous climb up the hill while our dog Max cowers behind my legs, tail beating the frozen ground, clearly anxious about the continuous disruption to our lives.

The truck, however, doesn't move. We watch, caught between apprehension and persistent hope, as it idles there for a moment or two at the bottom of the driveway, not even attempting to turn in,

BOTH FEET IN

and then the driver rolls down the window.

"We're not getting up that hill," he shouts up to us, his tone friendly but resolute.

Josh, jovial as ever, strolls down toward the truck, smile firmly in place, eyebrows raised in cheerful expectation. "Should we give it a try, at least?" he suggests, even though I'm pretty sure there's no *we* about this situation.

The driver shakes his head, his steely gaze on the steep hill. "Sorry, buddy, but it's not happening. I don't want to get stuck on that incline and roll back down. Not in my contract."

I decide to let my husband handle this one and, with my arm around Rose's shoulder, I start to shepherd my children inside. "Let's check out the house," I suggest cheerily, turning my back on the moving truck still parked stubbornly at the bottom of the hill.

"What happens if they can't get up the hill?" William asks. He sounds as if he's waiting for further information before he decides whether to worry.

"They'll figure it out," I state more firmly than I feel. The truth is, as excited as I've been to make this move, now that we're here, I'm feeling a little bit overwhelmed. Everything seems so *strange*—the empty sky, the endless woods, the silence save for the rumble of the moving truck's engine which suddenly cuts off, plunging us into a wintry stillness. That can't be a good sign, I think as I take the key to our house out of my pocket and fit it into the door's lock. I turn the key, open the door and step inside our new home, my children crowding in behind me.

For a second, we are all quiet, and I have a feeling we all forgot just how small it is. Of course, we've got tremendous plans for an extension—bumping the kitchen out over the hillside and expanding the living room out front with a big front porch besides, plus adding two bedrooms and another bathroom onto the side. We've already hired an architect and engaged a contractor and building crew, and they're going to start as soon as it's warm enough to live in a house that has one wall more or less open to the air for a significant amount of time.

But right now... this house feels kind of small and dark and musty, and I have to remind myself that we knew this, that it doesn't actually *change* anything.

"I forgot how amazing the fireplace is," I exclaim. It *is* amazing, taking up almost all of one wall of the living room, built of rounded stones, now blackened with smoke. I picture blazing fires with us all happily gathered around, toasting marshmallows or having a read-aloud of some worthy tome, because on top of the whole homesteading thing, we're also homeschooling. Major life changes all around.

"Which bedroom is mine?" Bethany calls as she wanders down the narrow hallway that leads to the three small bedrooms on the side of the house, overlooking the orchard. The other kids follow her, already jockeying for pole position when it comes to bedrooms, even though we'd already agreed back in New Jersey who got to sleep where. At least I thought we had.

I leave them to it and walk back to the kitchen, taking in the view over the sink of the gentle hill that rolls down to the little pond fringed with trees, before climbing ever upward. I fell in love with that bucolic sight when we toured the property less than two months ago, but it seems like an age ago now. For the last six weeks, we've been in constant motion—packing, giving away stuff, arranging the planned renovations, figuring out the unfamiliar shape of this new life of ours.

The bigger barn, I know, is full of tools and equipment Josh can't wait to figure out how to use. The moving truck at the bottom of the hill has, in addition to all our worldly possessions, stacks of books on how to garden, raise chickens, can vegetables, and milk a cow. If it's possible to learn how to homestead from a book alone, then I am certainly covered, but I have a feeling it's going to take more than a little book learning. Thankfully, I have the internet, too.

Now I stand by the sink, resting my hands on the cracked enamel, as I keep my gaze on the view of muddy yard, weathered barns and chicken coop, the glimpse of the pond beyond, its surface flat and gray under the wintry sky. *I live here*, I think, with a thrill of wonder—as well as a little twinge of terror. None of this feels real yet. I can't help but believe my suburban house outside Princeton is waiting for me, even though I put up the sold sign myself and vacuumed the dust bunnies from empty rooms. Still, I can't shake the feeling that this is nothing more than an Airbnb experience we might laugh about later, joking how we roughed it for once.

"*Mom!*" Jack sprints into the kitchen, skidding to a stop. "I am so not sharing a room with Willam. He snores."

I breathe in and out. We discussed the sleeping arrangements in detail back in Princeton, when it all seemed theoretical and all four of our children had their own bedrooms, although admittedly Rose's was tiny. But they knew they all had to share here, at least until the renovations were finished, which won't be until the summer, at least. They were all fine with it, back in Princeton. The reality, I know, always feels different.

"Jack." I turn from the view and try to smile. "There are only three bedrooms in this house. You know you have to share, at least for a few months."

"But not with William," Jack protests stubbornly.

I stare at him in amused exasperation. "Who then?"

"Rose—"

"I don't want to share with Jack!" Rose shrieks as she runs into the kitchen. "He's a boy and he *smells*!"

"I think something died in the closet of my bedroom," Bethany announces as she joins us in the kitchen, which is now feeling pretty crowded. "It smells like roadkill."

"How do you know what roadkill smells like? Do you go around *smelling* it?" Jack jeers, and Bethany just shrugs, unfazed.

"Okay, let's just take a breather from talking about bedrooms, okay?" I suggest. "First we need all our stuff." I strain to hear the hopeful sound of a moving truck laboring up the hill, but all is silence. Max whines, pawing the back door.

"What happens if the moving truck can't get up the hill?" William asks as he comes into the kitchen. I lean against the sink to give everyone more space.

"That's a good question." And one I don't have the answer to, but I hope Josh, my indefatigable husband, does. "Let's cross that bridge when and if we come to it," I tell William. "Why don't we look around outside?"

Everyone appears somewhat uncertain about this prospect, and I can't entirely blame them. It's cold and muddy and dusk is already settling over the trees, shadows lengthening across the tufty grass, but this is our life now, and we need to embrace it, including its many challenges.

"Come on, guys," I say bracingly. "Let's get the supplies out of the car, and then we can check out the barns and the pond. Explore!"

My voice rises a little manically, but at least nobody argues.

As we troop outside, I tell myself that a few blips are to be expected. I knew the shine would wear off the dream, as it so often does when we're confronted with the mundane and uninspiring aspects of whatever reality we've chosen. Once we unpack and actually start *doing* things, everything will look and feel better. Even if right now I'm not entirely sure how to start.

Once outside, we unload the boxes of food, dishes, and clothes I packed in the minivan so we wouldn't have to hunt through the many boxes from the moving truck.

I glance toward the bottom of the hill, and see that Josh is still talking to the movers, and he is now gesticulating wildly, his arms windmilling through the air. That doesn't seem like a good sign, and so I turn away. Still, I can't help but wonder, if the movers refuse to go up the hill, how will we get our stuff to the house? We can schlep the boxes for sure, but we'll definitely struggle with hauling some of the bigger furniture all that way. I'm not sure we'll be able to manage on our own.

It's a problem I decide not to think about now, heeding my own advice about crossing bridges, and so we head back into the kitchen where I unpack the coffeemaker, coffee, and milk for a much-needed cup, and the kids root around for something to eat. Maybe if I offer the movers coffee they'll decide to give the hill a try?

I am just digging out cups for this purpose when Josh comes into the kitchen. His hair is ruffled, his cheeks reddened with cold, and he has a look on his face that I know well. It's the determined smile of someone who is about to give me bad news and act like it's actually good.

"So," he states briskly, planting his hands on his hips. "The movers can't get the truck up the hill."

"Have they tried?" Bethany asks skeptically, and Josh's smile widens a fraction.

"No, but these guys are experienced, and they don't want to get stuck. Understandably."

William comes from the living room to stand in the doorway, his hands jammed in the pockets of his jeans. "So what are they going to do? Can they take all our stuff up the hill themselves?"

"Well…" Josh's smile falters, which alarms me. My husband's inexhaustible cheeriness is legendary. His smile never falters. "Apparently, that's not in their contract."

"What?" This from me, a sharp huff of disbelief. "Seriously?"

He nods, somber now. "Seriously. According to the contract we signed, if they have to walk more than a hundred yards we have to pay extra."

"Okay, then let's pay extra," I say quickly. If it's just a matter of money, then problem solved. After all, we need the movers to *move*. That's what they do, or at least, are meant to do.

Josh grimaces. "Yeah, well, I offered, obviously, but they weren't interested."

"But don't they have to…" I begin, but already he's shaking his head. "If we didn't specify the hill or the distance in the original contract, they don't have to agree to anything."

Briefly I close my eyes. Okay, so we need to figure out a way to move all our furniture and belongings up a steep hill in the oncoming dark by ourselves. This doesn't *feel* doable, but it can be. Hopefully. When I open my eyes, I see that Rose is looking anxious, Jack mutinous, William worried and trying not to be, and into the tense silence, Bethany asks what the point of having movers who don't move stuff is, which is exactly the question I'm asking myself. This feels like more than a blip, but we can still deal with it. We *will* deal with it.

"Okay," I say to Josh, forcing a smile. "So what do you think we should do?" I am considering calling another moving company, hiring local, hardy handymen, something that does not involve us carrying furniture that is way too heavy for us...

My husband flashes back the determinedly bright smile I know and love, but my stomach still swirls with dread, because I already know what he's going to say.

"We move it ourselves, of course."

Chapter Two

Outside it's getting dark, and the movers are having a cigarette break on the other side of the truck as we all troop over to it to survey its contents—furniture wrapped in padded blankets, a mountain of cardboard boxes and plastic crates, the occasional floor lamp sticking up like the neck of a giraffe. We got rid of a lot of our things when we moved from Princeton, since this house is so much smaller, but, as I survey the innards of the moving truck, I can't help but think that we clearly didn't get rid of enough.

Right now I am tempted to turn away from it all and just buy new, no matter how much that might cost. But of course we can't, first because we don't have enough money and second, because a lot of the stuff in that truck is sentimental. Also, if *this* truck can't get up the hill, who knows if any others will? Maybe we'll just have to live in an empty house, sitting on boxes and sleeping on the floor like... like *vagrants*.

For a second, no more, I feel an almost overwhelming longing to just go home.

This dilapidated cabin in the middle of nowhere is not home. This mud-encrusted stretch of nothing is not home. I don't know anyone here, I'm not sure I *want* to know anyone here, and the desire for the comforting ease of Uber Eats and Netflix is so strong it almost fells me.

What, I wonder with a despondency so deep it borders existential despair, on *earth* was I thinking, agreeing to this madcap, utterly absurd and idiotic plan?

"So, I think between William and me, we can manage the big stuff," Josh says in an almost aggressively jocular tone. "And Abby, you and Bethany can deal with the boxes and crates. Jack, you help William and me, and Rose, you're the linchpin when it comes to Mom and Bethany."

Rose wrinkles her nose. "What's a linchpin?"

"You," Josh says, giving her tummy a tickle, and I feel a sudden softening, a rush of love for this man who can remain relentlessly upbeat in the midst of my own self-absorbed despondency. It's Josh's superpower, and I need to catch some of its strengthening rays. I banish that wave of homesickness, and I give everyone a bracing smile.

"All right, let's do this," I say briskly, and Josh gives me such a grateful look that suddenly tears sting my eyes. My moment of self-pity completely evaporates in the light of what needs to be done. What *will* be done.

"Bethany..." I turn to my oldest daughter, smiling with the same determination as my husband's. "You up for this?"

Bethany lifts her chin, meeting my gaze. "Absolutely."

"Me too," William says, and Jack steps up to the truck, hands fisted on his hips.

"Yeah, let's do this," he says gruffly, sounding far older than his eleven years.

I love my family, I think with a rush of pride and affection. I love that they're up for this. That they know it'll be hard and they're still willing to do it.

"Okay," Josh says, "let's create a system."

And so, while the movers smoke their second cigarette, we start hauling all our worldly possessions up two hundred yards of semi-frozen mud.

The determined optimism and grateful love I felt when Josh convinced us all this can work lasts two whole trips up the drive and back before it starts to flag. The drive is steep and treacherous with half-frozen ruts of mud and loose gravel spinning away under my sneakers. My arms are aching, and it's getting dark—and cold. Very cold, with a frigid dampness to the air that seeps into my lungs.

Rose is trailing behind me, holding a single book that fell out of a box, and William and Jack are arguing about the best way to carry an end table while Josh referees. Bethany trudges along, silent and stoic, but also looking a little deflated. Still, we're doing it, I tell myself, and that counts for something.

And yet… the work seems to stretch ahead of us endlessly—not just loading this truck, but then unpacking the boxes, moving the furniture… and that's just *today*. What about when we get into all the *homesteading* stuff—am I really going to be able to raise chickens? Have a garden? Milk a *cow*? I was so excited about it before, and I am still, at least in *theory*.

In reality? It all feels incredibly daunting. I don't know the first thing about any of it, at least not *firsthand*, and when I think of all those serious homesteaders and preppers we've watched on YouTube, I am positive they would be rolling around on the floor laughing at us if they could see us now. Newbies. Greenhorns. Cosplaying the homesteading life. Cue the wondering shake of the head, the incredulous snort, the gleeful eye roll. *What were they thinking?*

And beyond all that, there's also the homeschooling to consider. Inside that truck is a crate of homeschooling books I've yet to so much as to flip through. I need to, though. I have four children who all have to be educated, including a daughter who needs to get her high school diploma in two months, and it's all up to me. Mostly, anyway. I am relying heavily on the internet, I confess, but we don't even have that hooked up yet.

In the dusky twilight, I head back to the truck, picking my way through the muddy ruts, trying to talk myself out of a rising sense of despair and even fear.

"Mommy, can we get a cat tomorrow?" Rose asks hopefully, walking so close to me that she almost trips me up as I turn from the truck, my arms laden with boxes.

"Maybe not *tomorrow*, Rose," I reply with an attempt at a smile. "But... soon." Maybe. At this point, I can't imagine adding a cat to the mix, but I know I probably will, along with the aforementioned chickens, cow, and who knows what else. That's why we moved here, after all.

I start up the drive as Josh and William attempt to haul our sofa out of the truck, with Jack dancing around them, eager to help but not actually doing anything.

"I can help too," Rose insists as the sofa lists precariously off the back of the truck. "Let *me* help."

Bethany glances back at them as she trudges up the hill with a box of dishes. "They're going to drop it," she announces with flat fatalism.

I glance at the movers, who are watching the whole scene unfold with a mixture of pity and indifference, not one of them so much as twitching a finger to help. Then we hear the rumble of an engine and the squeal of tires. In the twilit gloom, an old, battered pickup truck with headlights across the top of the cab pulls to a stop behind the movers.

"Y'all must be the new people who moved into old Jethro's place," a man says from the driver's seat, his elbow resting on the open window. I peer at him through the oncoming twilight, but I can't see much, although his southern drawl suggests he's a local. "Y'all look like you need some help with that," he adds before he turns off the engine and hops out of the truck, striding over to heft one end of the sofa and keep it from sliding into the mud.

"Thank you," Josh tells him gratefully. "Are you... are you a neighbor?"

"Sure am." The man beckons to William. "Slide over a little there, son, so you can get a good grip. And you—" He nods to Josh. "You're gonna have to do a squat to get this sucker down."

Obediently Josh goes into an alarmingly deep knee bend, and with the man directing, they manage to get the sofa out of the truck.

"This going up to the house?" the man asks, already starting up the drive with an arm of the sofa resting on one shoulder. He doesn't look particularly brawny, but he's wiry and strong, dressed in very dirty jeans, a well-worn jacket in red and white plaid flannel, and a baseball cap jammed on a head of brown, scraggly hair. He carries his end of the sofa with matter-of-fact competence, striding up the hill with obvious ease, like he's done it a million times before, and maybe he has.

"You don't have to..." Josh begins, *very* half-heartedly, because it's obvious that if we want the sofa in the house, this man does indeed *need to*.

"Well, you ain't gonna sit on the sofa in the middle of the road," he hollers, letting out the throaty laugh of a smoker before he purses his lips and sends a glob of tobacco-brown spit onto the ground, alarmingly near Rose's feet. She jumps out of the way, reaching for my hand.

"True enough," Josh replies cheerfully, after a millisecond's startled pause. "Let's get this up to the house, and then I hope you'll tell me your name."

As Josh, William, and our new neighbor head up the hill, the sofa resting on their shoulders, I glance at the movers and see they are looking a little abashed.

"I guess we can help with some of the boxes," one of them mutters, grinding his cigarette into the ground before he heads to the back of the truck to take a box of books. With a sigh, the other one follows. I feel a ripple of relief; we might actually get this done.

Bethany and I follow the others up the road, carrying crates and then depositing them inside the kitchen, where the boxes are starting to stack up.

The sofa is safely in our living room, and with Josh's help the stranger unwraps the padding from it and throws it, good-naturedly but with force, at one of the movers, who has to lunge to catch it.

"I'm guessing that belongs to you," the man says with a cackle, and then heads back down the hill. He's already pulling a chair out of the truck when Josh catches up to him.

"I'm afraid we don't even know your name," he says. "I'm Josh Bryant, and this is my wife Abby."

The man turns, still holding the chair, and gives a nod of greeting to us both. "I'm Henry Watkins, but most folks around here call me Hooch, on account of the moonshine."

"Mommy." Rose tugs on the sleeve of my coat. "What's moonshine?"

"Only the best stuff on earth, sweetheart," the man—Hooch—says with a grin as he pats the flask-shape lump in his pocket. "Now it's getting dark, and I reckon y'all want to have your gear inside." He nods up to the house. "So how about we get moving?"

With the help of Hooch as well as the movers, who have been shamed by him into doing their share, we miraculously manage to empty the truck in just over two hours. Hooch helps us unwrap all the furniture, and the movers take the blankets and padding back down to the truck and then beat a hasty retreat. They don't even hang around for a tip.

It's completely dark now, the first stars glimmering on the horizon. Josh turns to Hooch.

"I don't know how to thank you," he says, and Hooch grins, revealing a set of tobacco-stained teeth.

"Well, you could invite me in for some grub," he suggests with a grin. "I'm kinda hungry."

"Of course!" Josh exclaims, glancing at me for confirmation, and I nod. The frozen lasagna I brought for dinner can stretch to one more, certainly, and the least we owe Henry—Hooch—is a meal. "Come on inside," he adds, clapping him on the shoulder. "And thanks so much for your help."

"Well, that's what we do around here," Hooch replies cheerfully. "Help each other out. Except when we don't." He lets out a cackle of laughter that morphs into a mournful sigh and another spit of tobacco juice, this one thankfully not near anyone's feet. "Jimmy Taylor shot my dog, and I still haven't forgiven him for it. Said it was a fox, but he knew better, and anyway, he doesn't even have any chickens, so why'd he need to go and shoot a fox?" He shakes his head, spits on the ground once more for good measure, and then turns to us with another tobacco-stained smile. "Anyway, welcome to Wildflower!"

Chapter Three

Inside the kitchen Bethany and William help shift boxes so there is room to eat at the table while Rose clings to my side and Jack gazes at Hooch, clearly fascinated by this stranger. It would be fair to say we have never met anyone like Henry "Hooch" Watkins before.

As I put the lasagna in the oven, I give him a circumspect glance myself—under the single bulb of the kitchen light, he looks every inch what I guess he is—that is, a local. The word *redneck* floats through my mind but I quickly banish it. We didn't move here to be snobby, and Hooch has already proven himself to be a very good neighbor.

"So, y'all are city folk," he remarks, hooking his thumbs through the belt loops of his jeans. "From what I reckon."

I can't help but grimace in embarrassed acknowledgement, because of course it's obvious. Our ignorance and inexperience are hard-baked into everything we think and do.

"We're from New Jersey," Josh confirms with a nod. "Greenhorns, for sure. We're pretty new to this homesteading life."

"Homesteading, huh?" Hooch repeats, sounding doubtful, which is a little humbling, although understandable. Maybe true West Virginians, at least the country ones, don't even think they're homesteading; they're just living the way God intended them to.

"Well, you wouldn't be the first city slickers to come to the Mountain State and try your hand at the good life!" He lets out another one of his loud, cackling laughs that make us all jump, just a little. "We've got a couple right down the road from you who come all the way from San Fran Cisco." He draws out the syllables, making it sound like three separate words. "The Hoffenbergers. Been here for coming on five years, maybe? They were newbies when they started, yes sirree, but they know their way around the place now."

"We haven't met any of the neighbors yet, besides you, that is," I tell Hooch. "Who else lives in the valley?"

"In this here holler? Well, let's see…" He rocks back on his heels as he scratches the side of his nose. "There's little Lily Pepper and her husband Robbie. They moved here from Buckholt, oh, six months ago now? Bought Sam Miller's old place and are trying to fix it up, although Robbie don't know his ass from his elbow when it comes to carpentry." He gave a theatrical wince. "Begging your pardon, Miss, for the language."

"I'm afraid we might be in a similar way," Josh replied with a smile. "We're learning as we go."

"Well, that's all you can do," Hooch replies philosophically before resuming his spiel. "Now who else we got here? Well, there's Miss Barbara. She's been living up at the top of the road for about forty years, I'd say. Came to set up some sorta retreat, yoga or some such. She's a good one, even if she only eats veggies."

Bethany smothers a giggle at this, and I give her a look. She shrugs back, smiling, and I can't blame her for her amusement. Hooch really isn't like anyone we've encountered before, especially not in Princeton. I think we're all fascinated by him; he feels like a character out of a story, and yet already I sense he's probably the most genuine person I've ever met.

"There's a couple of empty cabins, too," he finishes. "Falling down wrecks mostly, from when people up and left 'cause they couldn't hack it here. Too bad the rats come in once they've gone."

At this Rose gives a little whimper of alarm. "*Rats?*"

"Yep, sure are, missy," Hooch replies with a certain cheerfulness. "They always come in when folks go leaving trash around and such like. Last ones to leave was the—now what was their name? The Johnsons, maybe? Barely out of college, those kids, and as for what they were growing in their veg patch..." He glances at Rose again. "Well, never mind about that. They didn't last the winter. Packed it in, hightailed it outta here in their old VW bus... left most of their stuff just lying around. And then the rats came." He says this last part with definite relish, and Rose shudders, although judging from her rapt look she's enjoying the story. Hooch tells it pretty well.

"Well, it's not the life for everybody," Josh remarks with a laugh.

"I reckon so," Hooch agrees with a somber nod, his face drooping so he suddenly looks a little bit like Eeyore. "We're pretty far out here, you know, for those city types who want to try their hand at homesteading. It's a good hour to Buckholt, and they ain't got much even there."

Not even a Target. I swallow hard. The words *what were we thinking* flash through my mind, but resolutely I push them away. It's time for positivity.

"Well, we're staying," Josh says firmly, sounding as positive as I want to be. "Where's your place, by the way?"

Hooch jerks a thumb behind him. "Just a little farther down the road, beyond the Hoffenbergers, right at the bottom by Sixpole Creek. Place gets flooded near on every spring but not much you can do about that. My great-granny moved there in 1922, just her and the six kids. My great grandpa was in the Battle of Blair Mountain. He was a genuine redneck, yessir." He straightens, giving us a salute and we all look surprised, because I don't think any of us has any idea what he's talking about.

Hooch glances around at us in a mixture of bemusement and disappointment. "You haven't heard of the Battle of Blair Mountain, I'm guessing?"

Josh shakes his head. "No, I'm sorry. Can you tell us about it?"

He doesn't need a second invitation. "*Well*." Hooch widens his stance, leaning back as he settles in to tell the story, his thumbs hooked through his beltloops. "Way back in 1921 was when it happened. Biggest armed uprising since the Civil War. My great-granddaddy, he was a coal miner down in Mingo County. It was a hard life, a very hard life. Down the mine all hours of the day, stooped over, breathing in that dust... and if you got black lung from it..." Hooch pauses, looking around at us all with sober expectancy. "Well, that's the end of you *and* your family," he proclaims. "Soon as you couldn't work, you were all thrown out on the street, even the little ones. Babies, too. They didn't care."

"But that's not fair," Jack protests, sounding outraged, and Hooch gives him a somber yet approving nod. "No sir, it sure isn't," he agreed. "And so the coal miners were trying to unionize like everyone else was back then, so they could have their rights—a working day that wasn't every hour God gave them. A paycheck that could feed their hungry little ones. An opportunity to buy from other places than the company store." He glanced again at Jack, and then at the rest of us, as serious as a schoolteacher. "Did you know that miners were only allowed to live in company-owned homes and buy from the company store? And I bet you can guess how flimsy those company-built walls were, and how *rid-ic-u-lous* the prices at the company-owned store." A sorrowful shake of the head. "And so then Mother Jones—you know Mother Jones?"

The kids all look at him blankly and I venture, "I've heard of her. She was a... union organizer?"

"She was, indeed," Hooch tells me with an affirming nod, and I smile, pleased by his approval. "She was eighty-three at the time of the Battle of Blair Mountain, eighty-three! But she never stopped." He pauses, rocking back on his heels before he continues his story. "Three thousand miners from Mingo County, my great-grandaddy included, were fired for joining the union and the mine corporation brought in agents from the Baldwin-Felts Detective Agency to evict their families from their homes—my great grandma was forced out by gunpoint with all her kiddies, and my great-grandaddy wasn't even at home to keep it from happening." For a second, anger sparks in Hooch's faded blue eyes. "Those agents threw all their gear right into the road, broke her wedding dishes into little pieces, and looked like they enjoyed it, too. My grandma and grandaddy and all their kids had to live in a tent along the Tug Fork River, and their house was left boarded up and empty."

"That's awful," I say quietly. I'd heard about such things happening, but only vaguely. Hearing it from Hooch made it all seem so much more real as well as terrible. I could practically see those broken dishes scattered in the dirt road.

Hooch nods solemnly. "The deputy chief, Sid Hatfield, was on the side of the miners. But when a scuffle broke out and an agent was shot he was brought up on charges. But Chief Sid Hatfield started something—there were skirmishes all up and down the Tug Fork

River during the trial, miners rising up to claim their rights, refusing to be ground under the heel of the Corporation."

He throws one arm up dramatically; all four of my children are now utterly rapt. Slowly Hooch lowers his arm, drops his voice. "The miners felt like they had someone important on their side," he explains quietly. "Finally. Hatfield was acquitted, thank the good Lord, and his name was in all the newspapers. But then he was arrested again later for dynamiting a coal tipple. That good man never stopped fighting, until…"

He pauses, lowering his voice further, while we all lean forward instinctively to hear more, spellbound by his story. "While he was walking up the courthouse steps accompanied by his good friend Ed Chambers," he says, practically whispering now, "those Baldwin-Felts agents were right there waiting at the top. And what did they do but open fire right on an unarmed man and his friend while he was heading to court. Not one person stopped 'em from drawing their Colt-made Thompson submachine guns on two innocent men." He pauses for dramatic effect.

"Did they…" Rose's voice is small. "Did they die?"

Hooch nods. "They did indeed, sweetheart. Hatfield was killed instantly. Chambers was riddled with bullets, fell all the way down the steps, and an agent came down and put another bullet in his head, for good measure."

"Goodness," I whisper, pulling Rose toward me. This story might give her nightmares, but I already know what Josh would say. *This is homeschooling right here. American history in the flesh!* And he'd be right, but it still feels a little gory.

"A terrible day," Hooch pronounced. "And the poor men had their wives with 'em! Those miners knew those murdering agents would never see justice. And so they started organizing—thirteen thousand marching on Logan County, my great-grandaddy included. It was the miners against the Logan County Coal Operators Association's private army. Those devils used poison gas and bomber plans left over from the war on those poor miners. They say maybe one hundred miners died on that day, and nearly a thousand were brought up on murder charges. My great-granddaddy was one of 'em. Spent the rest of his life in jail and made my grandma as good as a widow. But she was always proud of him, and that's a fact. He was a genuine redneck, yessir." Hooch nodded, while I glanced uncertainly at Josh. Interpreting my look correctly, Hooch explained with a kindly smile, "The miners wore red kerchiefs as a sign of their unity. They were called the Redneck Army. Now is that lasagna I smell? Because it sure smells delicious."

"Thank you for that story," Josh told Hooch, shaking his hand for good measure. "That's quite something."

"And yes, it is lasagna," I add, smiling. "Bethany, can you set the table? And William, get the milk out of the fridge? Rose, you can help Bethany. I'll just check the oven." It's nice to have something to do, to feel like we're making a home, a place where we can welcome people. And with Hooch's story about his poor great-grandmother being thrown in the street, I certainly feel grateful for the four walls and the roof we currently enjoy... even if I know there will be the Battle of Wildflower Valley tonight, about having to share the bedrooms.

Chapter Four

A dawn mist rolls across the meadow as I stand at the kitchen sink and fill the kettle with water. It's a little after six in the morning, and even though I'm exhausted from all the activity yesterday, I couldn't sleep. I had to get up and explore this new home—and life—of ours, by myself, in the quiet of the morning.

Last night was a busy blur; Hooch regaled us with more stories over dinner, eating three platefuls of lasagna while he talked almost nonstop. I'm not sure whether I should believe half of what he said, but he certainly loved a good story, and the children were enthralled as well as, it has to be said, a little taken aback by some of the more insalubrious details.

He told us stories of old-timers not being found in their cabin until they were nothing but bones, which made me feel like we'd moved to the outer reaches of Alaska rather than the backwoods of West Virginia. We weren't *that* far from civilization, surely? He also talked about the catfish and largemouth bass he'd fished out of Six-pole Creek, throwing his arms wide to show just how big they were. The huckleberries and juneberries—I'd never tasted either—that you could pick by the bucketful in summer.

"You've come to a slice of heaven, and that's a fact," he proclaimed, resting his elbow on the table as I poured coffee after dinner. "I'm not saying it ain't a hard row to hoe, because it surely is, especially when you're as green as you are. But if you've got grit and determination, you'll be all right. A little money doesn't hurt, either." He grinned as he raised his coffee cup in a toast. "Thank you kindly for this. That was the dang best lasagna I ever tasted."

"It's you we have to thank, Hooch," Josh said seriously. "We'd still be lugging our furniture up here if not for you!"

"I reckon you wouldn't have even got it off the truck," Hooch replied, and Josh gave a rueful laugh of acknowledgement.

Suffice it to say, none of us had ever met someone like Hooch before, and while he took some getting used to, he was someone I felt we could already count as a friend. When he said goodbye, he shook all our hands, gave Max a firm pat on the head, and promised to check in on us before too long, "to make sure the bears hadn't ate us."

"Bears..." Rose whispered, and I gave her a reassuring shake of my head.

"He was just joking, honey." At least I hoped he was. I knew there were brown bears up in the mountains, but it wasn't like we were surrounded by growling grizzlies.

"And I gotta make sure the greenhorns stick around," he added with a cackle of laughter before he bumped down the driveway in his truck, spraying up mud and gravel in his wake.

Josh and I didn't have much time to talk about our neighbor or his visit, since our house was full of boxes and the kids had started arguing about bedrooms the second Hooch was out the door, like they were on a timer.

"I am *not* sharing with Jack," Bethany stated, hands on her hips. She turned to appeal to me. "I'm trying to be adult and easy-going about this, but I am *eighteen,* and Jack is eleven. And a boy."

"And he farts," Willian interjected gloomily.

"*Everybody* farts," Josh pronounced in a jovial voice, and even I had to roll my eyes at that one.

"Okay, listen," I told Bethany, as well as my other three currently less-than-enthused children. "It's late, and everything's in boxes, so let's think of tonight like camping. Tomorrow we'll figure out bedrooms in a way that works." I gave them a can-do kind of smile. "All right?"

Amazingly, it worked.

"All right," Bethany said with a semi-apologetic smile, and William nodded, temporarily appeased.

Rose slipped her hand into mine. "Can I sleep in your room?" she asked hopefully. "I don't mind sharing."

"*I'm* the only one who was willing to share with anyone," Jack pronounced virtuously. He gave us all a quelling look. "Just remember that."

"Maybe that's because you're the one who farts," William muttered, before giving Josh a dark look. "No matter what Dad says."

Somehow we managed to find pillows and pajamas, sheets and blankets, and then make up the mattresses that we'd left propped against walls. The bedframes, currently in pieces, would have to wait till later. The kids got to bed, and Josh, with a devilish grin, withdrew a bottle of wine from his rucksack.

"Now *that* should have gone in the necessities box," I joked as he poured us both glasses. "Much more important than coffee."

"To us," Josh said as we clinked plastic cups of Chardonnay. "And to this." He nodded toward the house around us, dark and thankfully silent. The kids had, amazingly, gone to sleep.

"Are we crazy to have actually done this?" I asked as we sat perched on boxes in the darkened living room.

Josh cocked his head. "Maybe, a little?"

"Yesterday I watched a YouTube video about the seven things you must do before you buy a homestead."

"And what were they?"

"Walk the property line. Test the soil. Check about planning permits for properties that border your own. Meet your neighbors." I couldn't remember any of the others.

"Well, hey, we've met one neighbor and he was a hero," Josh replied with a smile. "We're newbies, Abs, and we're going to get a lot wrong. Everyone in Wildflower Valley will probably be laughing at how green we are, just like Hooch. But we're here and we're doing this, and that's what's important." He touched his cup to mine again. "So, cheers."

His confidence buoyed me. I was glad we did this, even if right now I felt nervous and more than a little afraid. "Cheers," I repeated softly, and drank.

Now, in the misty half-light of morning, I survey the rolling meadow from the kitchen window, still incredulous that this is my view, my *life*. As I wait for the kettle to boil, a deer creeps to the edge of the woods, glancing around warily with big brown doe eyes before she bends her graceful neck to nibble at the grass. A bird—I don't know what kind, not yet, but it's small and brown and bright-eyed—alights on a branch above her head and she startles, sees the bird, and then goes back to her breakfast. The bird surveys its domain for a moment or two before flying off with a graceful stretching of its wings into a sky that is still pink at its edges.

The kettle starts to boil, and I whisk it off the stove before its shrill can wake anyone up. I'm savoring this time by myself, when everything feels fresh and filled with promise. I'm also trying not to feel terrified, although I know the fear will kick in if I start to think too long or hard about all the things we need to do.

Till a garden. Build a fence. Fix the chicken coop. Get chicks. Figure out how to keep them alive. And then of course there's the unpacking, the figuring out how we are going to live in this tiny house until the renovation, meeting the neighbors, cracking open all the homeschooling books...

Okay, the fear has kicked in. I make coffee and pour myself a large mug, self-medicating with caffeine as I do my best to hold onto that nebulous feeling of excitement and possibility. Like Josh said, we're here and we're doing this. The question on my mind now is, what comes first? How do we actually *begin*?

I tiptoe through the kitchen, conscious of every creak of the floorboards, and into the living room where our sectional sofa that fit perfectly into one corner of our family room back in New Jersey now takes up over half the room. The other half is filled with boxes. Out the front window, the view of the hillside rolling down to the main road is covered in mist. A lone pine tree, halfway down the hill, lists alarmingly to one side. That was something else on the Seven Things To Do Before You Buy Your Homestead YouTube video, I recall. Survey all your trees and make sure they're healthy. Yet another thing that did not even occur to us to do before we bought this place.

I curl up in one corner of the sofa with my coffee, reminding myself not to panic. "We're here and we're doing this," I murmur to myself, like a prayer. "We're here and we're doing this."

"Mommy?" Rose appears in the doorway of the living room,

sleepy-eyed and tangle-haired, holding her worn blue teddy bear Bruce (she named him when she was two, and was very firm that that was his name) in one hand.

"Hey, honey. You're up early." It's not even six-thirty.

"Bruce couldn't sleep." Rose clambers over boxes to come snuggle next to me on the sofa. I put my arm around her and draw her close, breathing in her sleepy, child-like smell as she burrows into me.

"I guess he's getting used to a new place," I murmur.

"I think he misses New Jersey," Rose whispers, tucking her head under my chin.

"That's understandable," I tell her with an extra squeeze. This all has to feel very strange to a seven-year-old, no matter how excited we all were about the move. "Do you think Bruce might like to look around?" I suggest. "We could introduce him to the place, show him all around, and then maybe he'll feel a little more comfortable here."

"We could?" Rose perks up at this unheard-of suggestion. My usual MO in the morning is to fix my youngest a bowl of cereal and let her watch TV until she needs to get dressed. If I'm feeling virtuous, I'll limit the screen time to twenty minutes and then tell her to read a book. Whether I follow through on making sure she does is another matter.

But here we have no TV, no internet—yet—and more importantly, I feel different. I have a million things to do, starting with unpacking all the boxes currently surrounding me, but surprisingly in this moment I don't feel worried or hassled... well, not *much*.

"Sure we could," I tell my youngest child cheerfully. "We'll need coats and boots—it's chilly outside."

"Bruce doesn't have boots," Rose says, and from the gleam in her eye I know she's testing to see how far I'm willing to humor her when it comes to humanizing her teddy bear. I'm not about to dig out doll boots for him, though, if we even have them.

"Good thing he likes being carried," I say with a smile, and then scramble off the sofa, pulling Rose along with me.

We find boots and coats in a box in the mudroom, and with Max trotting faithfully behind us, alert to the possibility of an early morning adventure, we head outside into a chilly, gray dawn.

The ground is damp, the grass spangled with silver droplets of dew, the hazy mist just beginning to rise as we walk through the backyard, which is currently more meadow than lawn, to the big barn. We own eight acres, but only about two are cleared, and the rest is wooded hillside. Josh and I haven't talked too much about what we want to do with those wild acres; managing the two we have feels daunting enough.

Rose slips her hand in mind, Bruce dangling from her other, as we come to the first barn. I haven't been inside since we bought the place, and the door opens with a loud, creepy-sounding creak. I peek in, Rose half-hiding behind me, blinking in the dusty gloom. The barn is empty save for the machinery and tools Josh excitedly bought—in the dim light I see the bulky shapes of a post hole digger and a gas-operated tiller as well as a chainsaw, several shovels and hoes, a workbench and a wheelbarrow. He wanted to go whole hog and buy a tractor, but I put my foot down. A good one, I read online, can cost as much as one hundred thousand dollars. We were definitely not ready for that kind of investment.

Besides, we'd both agreed, as per the advice of the many homesteading videos and guides we'd watched and studied, to start small. "One mistake new homesteaders tend to make is they try to do too much too soon," Jane Do, one of the homesteading YouTubers we followed, proclaimed with an indulgent chuckle. "Buying the milk cow *and* the spring chicks *and* the tractor all in the first week!" Another chuckle, just to show how utterly stupid that would be. "What I like to tell those eager beavers is *slow down*. Start small. It's much better to learn as you go than bite off more than you can chew."

Knowing my husband, our definitions of starting small were bound to differ.

"Are we going to keep the animals in here?" Rose asks as she peeks around the barn door.

"What animals?" I tease. Josh isn't the only one who wanted to go all in right away. At dinner last night, William had pointed out that if we already had a dairy cow, we wouldn't have to worry about people having a second glass of milk. Which was true enough, but we might have to worry about where to put the cow or, you know, how to milk it.

"The cows," Rose exclaims, "and the chickens... and the sheep... and the geese... and the..." She frowns, clearly trying to think of some other animals.

"What is this, Old MacDonald's Farm?" I say with a laugh as I squeeze her hand. "And the chickens are going to go in the chicken coop! Should we check that out next?"

"Yes, let's!"

Grateful for my daughter's enthusiasm, we leave the barn for the coop next to it, which is small and ramshackle, made of seriously weathered wood with a corrugated tin roof that is peeling up at the eaves. Compared to some of the chicken runs I'd seen online, with individual nesting boxes and autofeeding systems—I never would have thought I'd be eyeing chicken coops enviously—this one was from another era. It was nothing more than a shed with a concrete floor and a smell of moldy straw.

"Look at the little door!" Rose exclaims, kneeling down in the damp grass to undo the latch on a little chicken-sized door next to the one meant for humans. So it has that too, and maybe that was all you needed? I supposed we'd find out. Buying spring chicks, along with tilling up some land for a vegetable garden, are the two top things on our to-do list.

"Pretty cool," I tell her. I peek in the second, smaller barn, Max sniffing at my heels, while Rose continues to play with the chicken door, letting her teddy bear Bruce slip in and out, giggling every time she closes the door on him. The smaller barn is empty, big enough to store feed and hay and whatever else we eventually decide; at this point, I have no idea what that would be. So much of this new life of ours still feels strange and completely unknown, like we're stumbling through the dark. *But we'll get there*, I tell myself. *We're here and we're doing this.*

I am just slipping out of the barn, Max bounding ahead of me, when I see Josh strolling across the yard. Dressed in a button-down shirt in plaid flannel and his heavy chainsaw pants, he is cradling a cup of coffee and smiling broadly.

My heart lifts at the sight of him and his obvious happiness. Regardless of how I feel about this move, or any lingering doubts that remain, I know that moving was the right thing for my husband and looking at him now, I'm so glad we did it... whatever challenges lie ahead, and, I already know, there are sure to be more than I could even imagine.

Chapter Five

"Having a look around?" Josh asks as he strolls up to me and plants a kiss right on my mouth. Clearly all is right with his world.

"Yes, Rose and I were showing Bruce around," I explain. "He's a little homesick."

"Ah." Josh nods knowingly. "Understandable." He glances around our property now glinting with morning sunlight. "What do you think?"

"It feels exciting," I reply and then add honestly, "and daunting. As it probably should."

Josh nods, unfazed. "I'm just trying to figure out what I want to tackle first."

"Well, the house," I say, reminded of the videos we both watched that all advised not rushing into anything. "Let's unpack, get the kids comfortable in their rooms, and then make a plan for the rest."

"Hmm." Josh does not sound convinced by my suggestion. Knowing him as I do, he probably wants to get the tiller or the post digger out and start breaking up ground or making holes or whatever it is he can do with those machines.

"But first, how about some breakfast?" I suggest. "And then we can make a plan."

"You and your plans!" Josh laughs as he wraps an arm around my shoulders, and I lean into him. "Okay, that sounds like a good idea," he says. "But first, why don't we have a little stroll around our very own homestead?"

His voice is buoyant with excitement and pride, and I smile. "You can give me the tour," I tease, glancing at Rose, who is still enraptured by the door on the coop. Who needs back-to-back episodes of *Bluey* when you have a chicken hatch to play with?

"Where should we start?" Josh muses.

"I've already looked in the barns," I reply. "Your tiller and post digger are waiting for you."

"But not the tractor," he mourns playfully.

"Not yet," I agree, with a sternness that isn't quite as playful. A hundred thousand dollars is a *huge* amount of money, and we're already spending more than I'm comfortable with on the house renovation. When I see the numbers on a spreadsheet, I start to hyperventilate. Yes, we made a lot of money on the sale of our house, but people spend their lives building equity, often to fund their retirement. Frittering it away on a dream isn't the wisest course of action, not that I'd phrase it like that to Josh.

In any case, on this morning, with the sunlight now streaming over the meadow, gilding every blade of grass in gold, it doesn't feel like time to fret or bicker about money or anything else. I want to enjoy the beauty of a new day as we start on this exciting life together, arm in arm.

We stroll together to the little pond behind the barns, its nearly perfect oval surrounded by slender white birches like something out of a fairytale. I can almost imagine a dryad—although I'm not exactly sure what a dryad *is*—emerging glistening from the silvery water.

We stand at the edge of the water, gazing down at its placid, albeit murky, surface. A few months ago, as we prepared for our epic homesteading adventure, we watched a video on taking care of any ponds or water sources on your property. We hadn't even bought this place yet, so it was all theoretical and I was helping Jack with his homework at the same time, but... I do recall a few of the main points—introducing friendly bacteria into the water to reduce algae blooms, aerating or adding oxygen to improve the life of fish, and keeping on top of fallen leaves and weeds. Now, as I glance down at the muddy stretch of water, barely glimpsing the mulchy depths of dead leaves on its bottom, it seems like we need to do all three.

But it's completely expected, I tell myself, to have a lot of work to do on this property, since it hasn't been lived in for the better part of a year. We can tackle it. We *will*.

We're here and we're doing this. I think I need that on a postcard, or maybe a poster, or even a tattoo.

"We'll have to find out what fish are in here," Josh muses. "And get a canoe or a kayak." You could probably paddle around the pond in five minutes, but yes, the kids will have fun with it. "And figure out if it has a natural spring. I wonder if this place floods? I remember what Hooch said..."

"But he lives lower down in the valley. Still..." I glance down at the ground, which is definitely on the muddy side. I'm glad I wore rain boots for this exploratory wander. What, I wonder, would happen if we flooded? I don't even know how to *begin* to handle that. Once again, I feel woefully ill-equipped. The locals will be laughing us out of town before we've even gotten started, or worse, after we have.

"Well, we'll figure it all out," Josh says cheerfully, like it's that easy, and I want to believe that it is. This is how we balance each other out; Josh dreams big, and I squish him back down into reality. We turn away from the pond and head over to the orchard—admittedly a rather ambitious word for a few fruit trees, but I like calling it that all the same—which was once enclosed by a rickety wood fence that is now mostly rotten.

"I'm pretty sure the realtor said these were apple and pear," Josh says as he rests one hand on the knobbly trunk of a tree. "And maybe plum. We'll find out soon enough, I suppose."

"Indeed." I study a tree, noticing that its knobbly bark is scorched black down the front. Was it burned by fire or struck by lightning or something else I can't even imagine? I am reminded yet again that another one of the points in that Seven Things You Should Do Before You Buy Your Homestead video was inspect all your trees. On eight acres, we have far too many to do that, but we could have at least looked at the ones that mattered, like these ones.

"Josh, what do you think this is?" I ask, pointing to the black mark on the tree's trunk.

Josh studies it, frowning. "I don't know... it looks like a burn mark."

"How would it have gotten burned?"

He shrugs, mystified and unbothered. "I guess we could google it... if we had cell reception or internet!" He laughs like he's made a joke, and I have to force myself to shake off my usual feeling of foreboding. A single black mark on a tree doesn't mean anything, I tell myself, even as I notice that almost all the trees in the orchard have it.

Never mind. We'll figure out what it is... and we'll deal with it.

I slip my hand into Josh's. I want to hold onto that happy, togetherish feeling that we had, strolling down to the pond. "Okay. What should we look at next?"

"The area for the garden?" he suggests, and we walk up to the overgrown meadow, mostly flat, east of the barns that we'd earmarked for our vegetable patch. Max trots behind, sniffing the grass eagerly.

"You'll have to get that post digger out," I say like a warning as we stroll the meadow's perimeter, fringed by beech and sugar maples. A quick check on the chicken coop shows that Rose is still playing with the little hatch, giggling all the while.

Josh and I both stand at the edge of the wild, untended space and survey it pragmatically. We've already agreed that the veg patch is the first thing we need to get going. It's already late March, and we'll need to start thinking about planting in early May if want to harvest anything this year.

Before that, though, we need to till the land and build a fence, which sounds a lot simpler and faster than I'm pretty sure it is. Looking at the tufty grass and the scattered, stubborn-looking and alarmingly large boulders that litter the ground, I have a feeling it won't be as easy as it was back in New Jersey, when our lawn was flat, the ground eminently tillable. And even then we didn't find it that easy.

"How big a patch were you thinking?" I ask Josh as he squints at the space in question.

"Hmm... I reckon we should start small." Thank goodness. "Maybe half an acre?"

"*Half an acre?*" I can't keep from yelping. "Josh, our garden back in Princeton was a third of that size, and I struggled to keep on top of the weeds." In fact I didn't keep on top of them, but miraculously, the vegetables grew anyway. We harvested an impressive number of them, some of which we still have, preserved in mason jars back in the house, but... back then, back there, it felt like a hobby. A game. There was always the ShopRite seven minutes away for the stuff we *really* needed.

This is real, and half an acre feels enormous, especially on top of everything else I need to do. I'm meant to be working twenty hours a week at my bookkeeping job starting next week, but right now I can hardly see how that might happen.

"You need one hundred and fifty to two hundred square feet of garden to feed one person for a year," Josh states seriously. "Half an acre is only a little over that. If we do half an acre this summer, we'll be keeping Rose and maybe Jack in food for the year. That's it."

"Yes, but we can't go from zero to sixty in a few seconds," I protest, and then clarify, "We can't go from buying everything at ShopRite to self-sustaining in one season, Josh."

"We won't be," he replies, imperturbable. "Like I said, half an acre would provide enough food for just one of our kids."

"Okay." I take a deep breath and let it out. I don't know why I'm letting the words *half an acre* freak me out. This is why we came here, after all. We can't homestead with a teeny-weeny garden, so I should be on board.

I *am* on board.

"Half an acre it is!" I sing out, and Josh smiles at me, looking almost tender.

"We'll take it one day at a time, Abs," he says. "I promise."

"Yes." I nod. "Definitely. So what's today's plan?"

Because, yes, me and my plans. I need one. Right now, all of the disparate elements of our new life feel like the boxes inside our house—taking up all the space and utterly overwhelming. Which one do you pick to unpack first.

"Breakfast?" Josh suggests, and I nod.

Breakfast I can do.

The mist has burned away as we head back to the house hand in hand, Max racing ahead and Rose running over to join us, the chicken door momentarily forgotten. High above us a bird—a hawk? A falcon?—soars against the empty canvas of a pale blue sky, its wide wings elegantly outstretched. The only sound is the chirp of morning birds and the wind whispering through the bare branches of the trees.

We're here and we're doing this.

I whisper it to myself one last time, and then, slipping my free hand into Rose's, I smile.

Chapter Six

Back in the house, we find Bethany curled up on the sofa with her book *The Complete Herbalist* opened on her lap. A couple of months ago, she indicated she had an interest in herbal remedies and wanted to do an internship at a local lavender farm rather than go, or even apply, to college.

At the time, I was more than a little alarmed. Bethany has always been incredibly driven, and for her to lose all her ambition so swiftly, like the air going out of a tire after you've driven over a nail, was unsettling to say the least. Parents always say they just want their kids to be happy, but I've come to realize that most parents—with me admitting to being at the top of that list—want their kids to be happy in ways they've chosen or at least approved of. Bethany, who had once been gunning for the Ivy Leagues, ended up choosing something for herself that I never would have, especially since I'm still not entirely sure what it is.

But moving to Wildflower Valley is part of her journey as well as ours, so hopefully we'll all figure it out together.

"Shall I start a fire?" Josh asks cheerfully. We stopped on the way from Princeton and bought a bundle of logs for ten bucks at a gas station. Josh told the kids this was definitely the last time we'd be buying wood, but I'm not so certain.

"Sure," Bethany replies, looking up from her book. "Where were you guys?"

"Just checking out the property. Lots to do."

Bethany looks around the box-filled living room as she shakes her head slowly. "I can't believe we actually did this. It feels surreal."

I know exactly what she means. Even as I go to the kitchen to find the eggs and bacon I brought from New Jersey, I can't shake the feeling that this isn't really my life. Maybe once we start unpacking, things will feel more permanent. Right now I still feel like I'm adjusting to an Airbnb. I can't find a spatula, there aren't enough lamps, and the rooms smell funny.

"Bruce is hungry," Rose announces as she follows me into the kitchen.

"Is he now?" I wonder how long this whole Bruce-is-really-Rose thing is going to go on, and whether I'm a bad mother if I don't tolerate it. "And what would he like to eat?"

"Cinnamon Toast Crunch?" Rose asks hopefully and I shake my head, smiling.

"We've got eggs, bacon, and toast," I tell her. "Perfectly good food for a teddy bear." Moving house seemed like the perfect opportunity to *stop* doing a lot of things, buying sugary cereals included. Even though I never meant for it to happen, a box of Cocoa Krispies or Cinnamon Toast Crunch so often ended up in my shopping cart. I couldn't even tell you why, only, I suppose, that in some way it made my life easier.

Rose's face falls but she accepts the inevitable, and heads back to the living room to curl up with Bethany on the sofa, Bruce tucked under her arm.

"What are you reading?" she asks, and I hear Bethany's murmur in reply, over the comforting crackling sound of the fire Josh has just laid in the fireplace.

As I break eggs into a bowl, I feel a sense of rightness settling inside my bones. It was for simple moments like this one that we moved, and I need to remember that, as I hold onto that feeling of peace that I know, for me at least, is still so fragile. Outside the mist has cleared away and the sky is deepening to a hard, bright blue. From my place in the kitchen, I can see the glint of water, the slender birches rimming the pond swaying in the brisk spring breeze. This still all feels surreal and uncomfortably new, but just a few hours in I feel like I'm not *finding* my groove but at least starting to sense it. Maybe.

By the time the scrambled eggs and bacon are ready, Josh and William have stumbled from their shared room, both of them grumpy because apparently, *both* of them snore. I let it bounce off me and give them extra bacon, which goes some way to restoring the optimistic mood of the morning. William broaches the idea of sleeping in the attic—an unheated, unfinished room that is our entire second floor, and I demur. I'm not ready to make any promises when it comes to bedrooms.

When the dishes are cleared and piled in the sink—there's no dishwasher, something I managed not to notice when we viewed the house but which I hope to rectify, because there's homesteading and then there's madness—I brew another pot of coffee and we all sit around our kitchen table, piles of boxes towering all around us, to Make A Plan, definitely in capital letters.

"So, I really think we need to tackle the house first," I start off firmly. Jack groans, Bethany nods, and William sinks his chin into his hand like he's already had enough of our family meeting. Rose isn't paying attention, and Josh is sipping coffee and refraining from saying anything, which worries me a little. I really want to get things unpacked.

"And after we've unpacked," William says, making it sound like that will take five minutes. "Then what? Can we get a cow? And chickens—"

"And a cat," Rose pipes up.

"Why don't we get a couple of sheep while we're at it," I quip. "And some horses and pigs and geese and..." I'm running out of animals.

"Pigs," William says seriously, "are not a bad idea."

"When can I get a gun?" Jack asks, and everyone swivels to stare at him.

"Please tell me," Bethany states in a deadpan yet fervent tone, "that you are not letting Jack anywhere near a gun."

"Not right away," Josh reassures her, and I feel like this conversation slipped away from me five minutes ago.

"Can we please," I ask, "unpack some boxes? And then we'll think about next steps." But not the ones Josh and my children are undoubtedly thinking about—like getting animals or driving the tractor we don't yet have. I'm thinking of things like getting internet, going grocery shopping, and checking in with my employer. I took two weeks off while we settled, but I can already see that that time is going to go by *very* fast.

"Of course, of course," Josh says soothingly. "We'll unpack boxes. We'll have to, if we want to be able to move around this place! And then maybe William and I can get the tiller and post digger going..."

"And me too," Jack adds, sounding a little disgruntled that he hasn't been included in this foray into big machinery.

"And you too, buddy, of course," Josh tells him, leaning over to ruffle his hair.

I'm about to remind everyone yet again that we need to be *practical*, when I realize I don't want to be the one to pour cold water over everything and dampen their enthusiasm. We just got here, and they're excited. We have a lifetime of practicality ahead of us, so if the boys want to play with their toys in the barn for a little while, maybe I should just let them.

Sure enough, Josh manages to unpack four boxes of clothes before he murmurs "I'll just go get..." and the next thing I know he, William, and Jack have all snuck out to the barn. I decide I don't mind, because the house was feeling crowded with all six of us in it—something that would alarm me, if I let it—and I can get more done by myself.

I manage to unpack all our kitchen stuff, or at least what we need for now. The NutriBullet stays in its box and goes down to the basement, along with the full set of fine china we never even used back in New Jersey, and a host of other implements that I still felt I had to keep even though I hardly ever got them out of the box before.

Rose wipes out the pantry shelves as I stack the food we bought—the remaining vegetables we preserved, and a few staples I'd packed so we don't have to head to town for a few days.

"This looks pretty good, doesn't it?" I tell Rose as I step back to survey our work. She looks around the narrow kitchen, frowning.

"It doesn't look like home." She regards me seriously. "Bruce doesn't like it."

Okay, I am definitely getting a little tired of the Bruce thing. "Bruce is back in your bedroom, so I don't think he can make up his mind yet," I tell her. "But we could use a few more homey touches." I tap my chin in thought. "You know what's missing? Our fridge magnets!"

About ten years ago, we started collecting magnets from every place we ever visited that sells a magnet—and you'd be surprised at just how many places do. Back in New Jersey, the doors of our huge sub-zero fridge were well-decorated with magnets. Here in our house in Wildflower Valley, the avocado-green fridge is decidedly smaller, and we'll struggle to get all the magnets on it. Still, I think it's a challenge Rose is up for, and I dig out the bag of magnets from another box and give her the job of decorating the fridge.

Then I go back to the bedrooms to check how Bethany is getting on unpacking her room. She's lying on her bed, reading her book; her clothes are already unpacked in the dresser, her corkboard of photos propped on top.

"I was going to hang it up, but I had no idea where Dad put the tools and stuff," she says without looking up from her book.

"I'm impressed. You had room for everything?"

She shrugs, her gaze still on *The Complete Herbalist*. "I got rid of a lot of stuff before we moved. And there are some boxes under the bed."

I perch on the edge of her bed, conscious of how much Bethany has sacrificed to move to West Virginia. Forget her prom, or even her graduation ceremony, or going to college or having a normal high school summer. She was willing to give it all up; in fact, after burning out pretty spectacularly last summer, she *wanted* to, but sometimes I still worry this move might be hard on her.

"How are you feeling about everything?" I ask.

"You don't need to worry about me, Mom," she drawls with a

faint smile. "I'm fine."

"I can still check in, though," I reply with a smile. "I know this is a lot to adjust to—"

"Yeah, how are *you* adjusting?" Bethany asks, looking at me over the top of her book. "Because, frankly, Mom, you were the one dragging your feet the most."

"I know I was." I can hardly deny it; everybody was on board but me for a good few months. "But reality is different than dreams, you know?" I continue. "And I wouldn't be surprised if every one of us had some doubts about what we're doing. That would be totally normal."

My oldest daughter looks amused, her hazel eyes so like Josh's crinkled at the corners. "I'm not having doubts, Mom." She puts down her book. "But I was wondering if, when we do the addition, I could have a stillroom? For my apothecary."

Stillroom? Apothecary? Has my daughter turned into a medieval monk? I'm not even one hundred percent sure what a stillroom *is*. "Talk me through your vision for a stillroom," I say, and she rolls her eyes.

"I know you think I got interested in all this stuff, like, five minutes ago—"

"Bethany, you *did* get interested in all this stuff five minutes ago." I keep my voice gentle. "That's okay. We all did, more or less. But right now I just want to... share your vision." I'm generally not one for that kind of corporate speak, but I'm trying to be encouraging.

"Okay." She lays her book aside and clasps her arms around her knees as she warms to her theme. "Well, I'd love to have a dedicated room to keep my herbs and stuff, and make you know—"

"Potions?" I half-tease and am rewarded with a small smile.

"*Tinctures*. And, um, infusions." She glances down at her book. "I think. I'm still learning—"

I hold up a hand to forestall her protests. "And that's okay. That's good. We're all learning, and we'll have to keep learning, a lot. So… a stillroom. How big would this room be?"

She frowns in thought. I'm guessing she didn't think I'd take her seriously, and I'm glad I have, even if our architectural plans have already been signed off. We might be able to make a little more space somewhere.

"Well, it wouldn't have to be too big," Bethany begins. "I mean, not a *closet*, but not like, a huge room. Maybe the size of a bathroom? With a table and some shelves for the different herbs, and some natural light…" She lets out an abashed laugh. "I don't know. I'm just reading about it all now."

"A stillroom sounds like a good idea," I say seriously. "Let's talk to Dad about it."

Bethany's eyes widen in surprise. "Do you mean that? Like, you'd actually consider it?"

"Why not? That's why we moved, right? To do these things? To be able to?"

"Yeah, but…" Bethany shakes her head slowly. "I feel like, back in New Jersey, you would just have given me a million reasons why it wasn't possible."

Ouch. I can't quite keep from wincing at that. Was I really that bad? That negative? With all the hassle and demands of our former life, I probably was. And this life isn't necessarily going to be easier; in fact, in a lot of ways, it's going to be so much harder. But at least I can say yes to my children's dreams. Well, some of them. We're still not ready to get William's milk cow, or a gun for Jack. Definitely not.

"That may be," I tell Bethany, "but now I'm saying it is possible. At least, it might be. We'll have to look at the plans and see where we can make room."

I am rewarded by my eighteen-year-old daughter doing a very uncharacteristic thing and throwing her arms around me. "Thanks, Mom," she says, and as I hug her back, I feel that sense of rightness settle inside me again, and it's welcome.

We're just pulling away from each other, smiling in a slightly sheepish, damp-eyed way, when someone knocks on the front door, three loud raps that sound like whoever is there means business.

We have visitors.

Chapter Seven

Rose is just coming out of the kitchen, her arms full of magnets, as I hurry to the front door, patting my hair because I have no idea what I look like, and I haven't so much as glanced in a mirror all day. I don't think I've even brushed my teeth.

"You look fine, Mom," Bethany whispers from the doorway of her bedroom. "Maybe just smooth your hair down in the back. Looks a little like a bird's nest back there."

Hastily I follow her suggestion as I paste a smile on my face and then open the front door.

"Hello—"

"He-*llo*." The woman standing on the front porch is already making her way past me inside, pushing me aside with a firm elbow. A man lingers on the porch, looking sheepish. They both look to be in their sixties, trim and fit and silver-haired, and are wearing a variety of upscale activewear in hardy-looking Lycra. I think I already know who they are—the Hoffenbergers, whom Hooch told us moved from San Francisco five years ago. They started out as newbies but clearly have found their feet and then some.

"Hi, I'm Abby Bryant," I say with friendly pointedness as the woman strolls into our living room uninvited, glancing around in obvious speculation.

She turns around, her eyebrows raised, her lips curved in a knowing smile. "Oh yes, we know who you are—"

"I don't think she knows *our* names, honey," the man says with a laugh. He's standing in the doorway, rubbing the back of his neck. "Pardon my Allie," he tells me. "She was excited to get some new neighbors."

"Oh, Lord!" The woman laughs and shakes her head. "Sorry I didn't say. I'm Allie Hoffenberger, and this is Bill, my husband. We moved to the homestead next door, about a quarter mile down on your right toward Sixpole Creek, five years ago. Welcome." She sticks out a hand, and I shake it. Her hand is small, but her grip is firm.

"Nice to meet you," I say. I already get the sense that the Hoffenbergers, and in particular Allie, are going to be a friendly force to be reckoned with.

"We brought some housewarming things over," Allie says. "Bill, get the box from the truck."

Bill heads back outside while Allie looks around, her eyes narrowed in assessment. "This place *is* small, isn't it? Of course it was just Jethro up here. Jethro Tucker. Did you ever meet him?"

"No, it was empty when we viewed it—"

"He up and left about a year ago now," Allie confirms with a nod. "Went to live with his daughter down in Florida. Had enough of the grind, I guess! He kept it pretty nice and tidy, though, but..." She blows out a breath as she shakes her head.

"A year is a long time for a place to be empty, especially out here in the woods. We have hard winters here, you know, and I think the roof of your barn is just about falling in." I didn't think it was *that* bad, but before I can reply she continues with a cluck, "You'll have your work cut out for you, for sure."

She gives a little nod, her hands planted on her hips, before she spies Rose half-hiding in the kitchen doorway and asks in a chirpy voice, "And who's this?"

"This is Rose, my youngest." I walk over to steer my daughter out of the kitchen with one hand on her shoulder. Rose mumbles a hello. "And Bethany," I call meaningfully, and my oldest daughter emerges from her bedroom, smiling uncertainly, her book clutched to her chest. "My oldest."

"My, my," Allie says by way of greeting.

I'm not sure how to take that, so I just keep going. "My husband Josh and my two sons William and Jack are out in the barn. We also have a dog, Max."

"Six of you in this place?" Allie's eyebrows rise skeptically, like she can't believe we can cram ourselves in here. Well, I can't really believe it, either, but here we are.

"We're planning an addition," I tell her. "As soon as the weather warms up a little we'll be good to get started."

"Oh my." Her eyes widen as she gives another one of her head shakes. "You've already got planning permission for that, I hope?"

I'm not sure what business it is of hers, but I smile and nod. "Oh, yes. It's all been approved." Thanks to Josh and tireless hours of filling out and filing forms. The builders have already come and marked out the foundations. We're hoping the whole thing will only take a few months, but I am pragmatic enough to recognize that might be wishful thinking.

"Well, then." Allie gives another nod, her beady gaze moving around the crowded living room, taking in the sofa, the stacked boxes. I can't tell what she thinks of any of it, but I have a feeling it's not particularly good. "Henry told me you were from the city?"

she asks, her gaze still moving around the room.

For a second, I don't know who she means, and then I realize she's talking about Hooch.

"I don't know about the *city*," I tell her with an attempt at a laugh. "We're from just outside Princeton, New Jersey. And I think he mentioned you were from San Francisco?" My tone is the tiniest bit pointed. If anyone's from the city, surely it's her and her husband.

"That's right. Bill and I both worked in tech for years, but we decided to give it all up for proper living." She smiles. "It's a steep learning curve, but you'll figure that out soon enough if you haven't already."

I know she's being friendly, but there's a hint of know-it-all smugness to her tone that irritates me a little, although I try not to show it. The Hoffenbergers are our nearest neighbors, after all. According to the YouTube videos we watched, these are the people we'll need to depend on when the power goes off, or the truck we don't yet have breaks down, or one of our kids breaks their leg and has to be rushed to the hospital. All the crises we have to look forward to, to be weathered with the help of our salt-of-the-earth neighbors.

"I'm sure you have plenty of stories to tell," I remark, and Allie Hoffenberger's chest swells up as she nods emphatically. I brace myself for her to launch into a monologue about just how much they've learned over the last five years.

Before she can say a word, though, her husband Bill comes through the front door, carrying a large cardboard box.

"Ah, here he is!" she exclaims instead. "Where can we put this down?"

I direct them to the kitchen, and follow Bill in, watching as he heaves the box onto the table with a clunk.

"Now let's see what we've got here," Allie says, and starts unpacking the box herself. "Wild huckleberry jam, I made it myself last August. Preserved peaches—we have our own orchard, you know. This tomato relish goes well with most meats. Bill wouldn't eat a sandwich without it, and that's a fact." She chuckles before resuming her inventory. "Applesauce from our own Golden Delicious apples—West Virginia's state fruit, in case you didn't know—and this..." She brandishes a bottle filled with a deep purple liquid. "Our own blackberry wine! Hooch's moonshine isn't a patch on it, and that's a fact."

"Thank you, this... this is so kind," I stammer, but there's more in the box.

"Now I don't know what we would have done without these," she tells me, and takes out a few weathered pamphlets. "They're from the National Homesteading Association, and they really are godsends. Short and sweet, because you can get bogged down in so much information, can't you? *We* don't need them anymore, of course, but I thought you might appreciate them, since you're just starting out. There's everything here from keeping chickens to preserving vegetables to building a fence. Whatever you need to know, you'll find it in here." She waves the pamphlets in front of my nose.

It's all valuable information we could use, and yet something about her manner seriously grates. I'm trying not to let it show, but I must not succeed because Bill says, with a slightly apologetic smile,

"They might know more than we did, Allie, back in the day." He's clearly used to his wife's kind-hearted bossiness.

"Don't be ridiculous, Bill," Allie exclaims. "They clearly have no idea what they're doing. They bought this place practically sight unseen, and they were living in the *city*. I bet they don't know the first thing about homesteading."

Okay, maybe scratch kind-hearted. "Well, we did actually tour this place," I feel compelled to reply. "So not *exactly* sight unseen—"

"But did you notice that every single tree in the orchard has fire blight?" Allie demands. I stare at her gormlessly while she fills in a little pityingly, "it looks like scorch marks down the trunk of the tree. If it's detected early, it can be treated, but those trees have had it since before Jethro left. I'm amazed they're still standing. They'll need taking down, for sure, because of course fire blight spreads through spores on the wind. You'll be lucky if you don't have to chop down every tree on your acreage. And you'll need to burn the wood far away, to prevent contamination. Thank goodness we haven't had it yet." She speaks meaningfully, like if they get it she'll know who to blame, and I guess they will. I am reconsidering my whole view of this woman, because right now I have a feeling the main reason she came here was to show me how little I know.

Once again, some of my feelings must show on my face because Bill jumps into the breach. "Now, now," he says placatingly. "Allie, you know as well as I do that fire blight mainly affects fruit trees." He gives me a kindly smile. "Many of your trees shouldn't be affected. And the ones that have it only a little, you can manage by pruning the infected branches. It's not as gloomy as all that, especially if you act quickly."

"But their whole orchard has to go," Allie declares with something that looks like a satisfied nod. Maybe she's pleased the greenhorns have revealed their utter inexperience.

"Well, I guess we'll have to look into it," I say, trying not to sound as poleaxed as I feel. *Our whole orchard?* I think of the hope I felt when Josh and I surveyed it this morning, imagining basketfuls of apples and plums, pies and cobblers and jam. I saw those scorch marks and even though I worried about them, but I had no idea it meant *all* the trees were, it seems, diseased and basically dead.

"You certainly will," Allie says with emphasis and Bill murmurs, "Now, Allie…"

A silence falls on us, and Allie looks at me expectantly. She has bright, beady eyes like a bird, and a neat silver bob she tucks behind her ears. Her sense of brisk capability and assured knowledge makes me feel woefully insecure, playing as it does on all my fears that we are in over our heads and no matter that we said we're here and we're doing this, maybe we shouldn't and can't.

But instead, to my own surprise, I find myself feeling the opposite of all that. I straighten a little, throwing my shoulders back in a way that makes Bethany, lingering in the doorway, lift an eyebrow, and face my new neighbor directly.

"We have a lot of things to look into," I tell the Hoffenbergers, but mainly Allie. "And, as you can tell, we're totally new to this, but we're learning every day, and we *will* get there." I give Allie a steely smile. "Thanks for the heads up about the orchard. We'll have to have you over for dinner once we're unpacked."

I don't *think* I meant it to sound quite as final as it did, and belatedly I realize I should have probably asked if they wanted a cup of tea or coffee, since they came all this way, *and* bearing gifts. If I'd been really organized, I would have had a plate of home-baked cookies to go along with it, and the house would be in a far better state than it is.

A beat of silence follows my words and then Bill says, in his mild, semi-apologetic way,

"We should get out of your way. Allie just couldn't wait to come over and see who'd moved in so close to us. There aren't that many of us around here, you know. Just you and Henry and the Peppers, and they're just a couple of kids." He smiles at me, an almost pleading look in his kind eyes, while Allie busies herself taking out the last few things from the box—a paper sack of homemade scone mix, and a plate of ginger snaps swathed in plastic wrap.

Okay, now I feel like a total heel. Allie isn't looking me in the eye, and I have a terrible feeling I hurt her feelings. It could be, I consider, that her bustling, bossy attitude hides a heart of gold, or maybe just one that's lonely.

"I know our house is a mess," I tell them both, "but if you'd like to stay, we could have a cup of tea with those ginger snaps you've made. They look delicious."

"Well, I wouldn't want to intrude..." Allie begins with a sniff.

"Oh please, I insist," I say firmly. "You're our neighbors! And I'm sure we could learn so much from you." I turn to Bethany. "Why don't you call in Dad and the boys? They'll be ready for a break by now."

Bethany gives me an inscrutable look before nodding and heading outside.

I smile at Allie. "Please," I say again, and finally she seems mollified.

"Well, if you *insist*," she says, like she's doing me a favor, and I hide my smile. I think I might have the measure of my tricky but kind-hearted neighbor... at least I hope I do.

Chapter Eight

Four days into our Wildflower Valley life, the house is mostly unpacked, and Josh is tilling up the meadow. At least, he's trying to. I watch him from the kitchen sink, doing my best not to worry about his progress. He and William have been out there since seven o'clock this morning, and let's just say half an acre seems eminently *un*doable right now.

I'm trying not to let my spirits flag, but since we've moved, it's felt like we've had obstacle after obstacle to overcome. First, the apple and plum trees in the orchard, every single one with a scorch mark. Once the Hoffenbergers left—after a cup of tea and plenty of advice about everything from planting a vegetable garden—"I hope you're not planning on doing it on that meadow out there, with the hillside drainage it will be a *nightmare*"—to buying livestock—"Forty meat chickens should be enough for your family, but you need the space, and I wouldn't even *think* about cattle yet"—Josh and I walked out to the orchard to inspect our diseased trees.

"They've all got it," I said flatly, fighting futile tears. Twelve trees in our little orchard, and every single one with the dreaded fire blight. I'd tried to google it on my phone, but of course we don't have signal, something that seemed like a blessing this morning, but now was definitely a curse, or at least a serious annoyance.

Josh was quiet for a few minutes, longer than he usually was, as he surveyed the blighted trees, his hands on his hips.

"Well, we'll just have to plant new," he finally said resolutely. There was a slight tremor in his voice, and I knew he was fighting his own disappointment, just as I knew he felt he had to hide it from me. "And," he continued with a trace of his old enthusiasm, "we'll get to plant what we want! Cherry or pear or peach..." He trailed off, looking at me expectantly, waiting for me to pick up the slack, which I duly did, because what choice did I have?

We're here and we're doing this.

"I think I'd like a peach tree," I said, and Josh grinned with relief.

"Yeah, peach, definitely," he agreed, and we both stared at each other, seeming to silently acknowledge both our fears and determination.

The fire blight, however, was just the first obstacle. The next came when we called an internet service provider and discovered we were in something I'd never even known was a thing, which is the National Radio Quiet Zone, a thirteen-thousand square mile area between the Green Bank Observatory and the Sugar Grove Research Station that limits wireless communication, i.e., the internet. I was starting to understand why we didn't have cell phone signal... but *internet*?

"No internet?" I goggled at Josh after he'd gotten off the phone with the internet service. "No internet at *all*?" It was like he'd told me we'd be living without electricity or running water. He basically had.

"Not at *all*," he said quickly. "It's just a little trickier to set up than we might have liked. We can use a roaming service which will be patchy or sign up for a satellite service, but apparently there's a waitlist for that. It'll be..." He paused while I braced myself. "Six weeks or so."

"Six weeks!" I practically screeched. "Six weeks with no internet?"

"Come on, Abby," Josh pleaded. "It's not that bad."

"What about homeschooling?" How could I teach without the internet? "And my *job*?" I needed text, email, Zoom, all the online tools of the remote worker. At that moment, as pathetic as I knew it made me seem, I could not imagine functioning for that length of time without the internet. "And what about YouTube?" I added. "We need to watch all those tutorial videos. We need to google all kinds of stuff..."

"It's only six weeks, Abby." Josh sounded tired, and so I stopped. Rallied, as I knew he needed me to. Again.

"Okay," I said with an attempt at optimism. "We can make it for six weeks. And," I added with a smile, "we have books, after all. Old school." I'd just have to go out to work, somewhere with internet, maybe in Buckholt.

"Yeah." Josh grinned, clearly relieved. "Old school."

So no orchard and no internet, I thought, but we could still make progress. I encouraged Bethany to start working toward her high school diploma; we'd met with the guidance counsellor at her high school before we'd left and arranged for her to do her work remotely, since she only had two months until graduation. Bethany, however, seemed more interested in reading *The Complete Herbalist* and using an app on her phone—one that fortunately (or not) didn't require a signal—to design her stillroom.

I dragged out the books I'd bought for Rose—Saxon Math and Shurley Grammar and a host of others that looked intimidating even though they were meant for first grade—and then put them away again. "We'll start next week." I told her, and she grinned, happy enough to leave the books aside.

I didn't even bother getting Jack's books out. As Josh had said more than once, *this* was their education, even if right now Jack's education consisted mainly of throwing rocks into the pond and begging Josh to let him use some of his power tools.

I glance out the window again; Josh has stopped the tiller once more, thanks to a large rock that he and William are attempting to dig out. There are a lot more rocks in our pleasant little meadow than any of us realized, often hidden under the tufty grass. It's amazing how you don't notice rocks until you decide you want to plant a garden. A sigh escapes me, and then I straighten, not wanting to start feeling anxious.

As Josh said, as I *knew*, there were bound to be blips. So far, we've navigated them all... more or less. We still need to deal with the trees in the orchard, and I start work tomorrow, without internet. I'm planning on driving to Buckholt to work in the library, but that leaves Josh alone with all four kids which *should* be fine, but... may not be.

Besides, there are some positives, I remind myself. The contractors are coming next week to officially start the addition, after having done some pre-construction work, mapping out the foundations and bringing in building materials, before we moved.

And yes, that also means we'll be living in a building site, but... progress. Plus, the Hoffenbergers invited us over to dinner on the weekend. I offered to bring something, and Allie patted my arm and assured me that she liked to do all the cooking herself. I felt like that kind of comment set the tone of our neighborly relationship, which is fine, because we're all friendly and I'm just as happy *not* to bring something. Sort of.

We still haven't met the Peppers or Miss Barbara, the other Wildflower Valley residents, and I keep meaning to walk up the road to their homes, but I haven't managed it yet. There's enough going on right here to keep me busy, anyway.

The sound of the tiller's motor revving again has my spirits, or at least my hopes, lifting once more. Then I hear a sound that definitely isn't good—something between a grinding and a crack, and then the motor cuts down and Josh swearing out loud echoes through our little slice of heaven.

Oh, dear.

I make for the backdoor as Bethany sticks her head out of her bedroom.

"What happened?" she asked, eyes wide, because Josh never swears. Well, hardly ever.

"I think it's a problem with the tiller."

"You mean with the rocks," Bethany replies, and I sigh and smile at the same time.

"Yes, with the rocks."

"Can you please ask Rose to contain her toys?" Bethany asks as I open the back door, clearly *not* choosing her moment. "She set up an entire doll city on the floor." Her voice is needled with irritation. "I can barely walk to my bed."

Back in Princeton, we had a playroom—a dedicated space for toys, video games, Lego constructions, craft projects, anything noisy or messy that I could close the door on and happily forget about.

That is not the case here.

"I'll talk to her," I tell Bethany, and irritation needles *my* voice, because can't she see I'm busy? She mutters something as she stomps back into her room and I head outside to where Josh is crouched down by the tiller, inspecting the motor. William is still trying to shift the large rock. This doesn't look good.

"What's up?" I ask lightly. The weather is a little warmer today, with a gentle breeze that reminds me spring is almost here. The birches by the pond have the tiniest little buds starting to form, bright green and hopeful. The grass is turning greener too, much of it churned up under Josh and William's efforts.

"I hit a rock," Josh replies shortly. "I bent one of the tiller blades."

"I'm sorry." I pause as I stand at the edge of the meadow, the wind ruffling my hair. "Can it be fixed?"

"I don't know." He sounds irritable, which is so unlike him. Four days in and we're all feeling a little tetchy. Well, I remind myself yet again, it was bound to happen. We'll get past it.

"We can always do it the old-fashioned way," I suggest. "*Little House on the Prairie* style."

"What, with a couple of oxen and a plow?" He still sounds irritable.

"Actually, I meant a gardening fork and a rake," I reply lightly. "And our muscle."

Josh is already shaking his head, his gaze still on the bent blade. "That would take way too long."

I glance at the half-tilled meadow—not even half, I acknowledge, and not even a third. William is still trying to lever a rock out with a shovel, doing his best to put some muscle into it with his shoulder. I glance back at Josh.

"Well, what are our options?" I ask, trying to be practical.

"Buy another tiller?" he suggests, an edge to his voice. I'm not sure if he's serious; the one we have cost five hundred bucks. "Or figure out how to fix this one," he continues on a dispirited sigh, "and frankly I have no idea how to do that." He slaps the side of the motor and then straightens, running a hand through his hair as he gazes moodily off at the hillside.

I'm pretty sure what's happening here, I realize. Josh is coming up against his own inexperience and ignorance and it *hurts*. I think I've been plenty aware of mine all along, but I suspect my husband believed that positivity and a willingness to learn would carry him through. And maybe those qualities will, eventually... but it will take a lot of moments like this one. Recognizing our deficiencies and figuring out a way forward.

"We could take it somewhere," I offer hesitantly, trying to find that way forward. "To the feed store in Buckholt? I think they might do machine repairs." Back in Princeton, we looked up all the businesses in Buckholt, figuring we'd be frequenting them fairly regularly, and there was definitely a feed store.

"And pay a hundred bucks to fix something that cost a little more than that?" Josh asks with a huff.

"Well, kind of a lot more—" I begin, before Josh silences me with a look that is a borderline glare.

"Abby. I don't want to do that."

"Okay." I meet his glare with a level look of my own. In every marriage, you learn to balance each other out. When one person goes high, the other goes low, and vice versa. Right now, I need to be the steady one, even though that's often Josh's role, dreamer that he is. When the dream starts to waver, he can get a little emotional. Now looks like it is one of those times.

"Well, if you don't want to fix it," I say, knowing I am stating the obvious, "then we either have to borrow someone's or buy a new one, or do it by hand. Right?"

"It's these rocks," Josh bursts out. "There are so many of them. And the soil isn't like it was back in New Jersey."

"I know." West Virginia is known for its fertile soil. The Monongahela silt loam is actually the state soil—I didn't know there was such a thing—and is deep and well-drained and considered prime farmland.

We do not have Monongahela silt loam here in Wildflower Valley. What we have, up here on the hills, according to the Hoffenbergers and confirmed by the soil test kit we'd bought, is a soil called residual, that comes from sandstone and shale, is acidic, and has moderate to low fertility.

And apparently, due to the number of rocks, is hard to till.

Josh is still staring at the tiller, his hands on his hips, while I stand there, trying to figure out a way forward and having no idea what it is.

William straightens from where he's been futilely trying to move a boulder. "Hey," he calls to us. "It's Hooch."

I turn to see our neighbor striding from the front of the house, the brim of his baseball cap pulled down low. He's wearing the same thing he was the last time we saw him—a red and white flannel jacket and dirty jeans.

"Howdy, strangers!" he calls to us. "I thought I'd check on y'all, which is a good thing, since it looks like you need some help."

Chapter Nine

The next morning, it feels almost surreal to drive into Buckholt; since we've moved, I haven't left the property once. And while five days might not seem like much time at all, trust me, when you've been without internet, cell phone service, or civilization in any significant capacity, it is.

Yesterday Hooch came to our rescue, if in a roundabout way. I think we'd all hoped he might be able to fix the tiller with a pocketknife and a bit of twine, like some kind of redneck MacGyver, but after inspecting it alongside Josh, he merely confirmed our suspicions.

"Yep, looks pretty busted to me," he announced as he straightened up. "You can replace the blade easy enough, but I'm guessing the motor's conked out as well. You want to take it to Robbie Pepper. He might not know the first thing about farming, but he's a pretty good mechanic."

"Even if I fix it," Josh remarked wryly, "I might just go and break it again on all these rocks."

"Yep, there are a fair few rocks here," Hooch agreed, scratching his cheek as he looked around our poor meadow. "The only way to get those suckers out is with some elbow grease. I can help, if you like, with some of the bigger ones. I gotta be in Buckholt by six for dinner with my sister Daisy so I got some time."

While I went to get coffee and cookies for sustenance, Josh, Hooch, and William levered out the bigger rocks from the meadow. It took all afternoon, and while I know Josh was immensely grateful—as we all were—I think he felt humbled and maybe even a little humiliated that he needed so much help, so soon. If we weren't careful, we'd end up like Robbie Pepper, who, mechanic though he might be, didn't know his ass from his elbow when it came to homesteading.

Neither, it felt like, did we.

Fortunately, Hooch had some further suggestions. The Hoffenbergers, he told us, had a motorized tiller that was "a heck of a lot bigger" than the "puny lawnmower" we had, and he thought they'd let us borrow it. I was wary of borrowing anything from the Hoffenbergers, and I think Josh was too, but Hooch was insistent—so insistent, in fact, that he drove to the Hoffenbergers' place himself, got the impressive-looking tiller, and brought it back in his truck.

"That's the way we do things around here," he announced cheerfully after he'd unloaded it. "Now just make sure you don't break this one!" He laughed heartily at that, slapping his thigh, and then took a cookie for the road before heading off.

Josh and William are planning to finish the tilling today, while I'm at work, and I am praying they don't break the Hoffenbergers' snazzy machine. I know Josh has been trying to maintain a positive attitude, but the difficulty of getting the ground tilled has definitely dispirited him.

"I guess I just wanted one thing to be easy," he confessed to me on a sigh last night. "And to go and break the thing the first time I used it…" He shook his head, his mouth tightening with self-contempt.

"I think," I told him as I put my arms around him, "in this life we've chosen, there are a lot of times when we're going to feel stupid."

"Yeah. I know you're right." He returned the hug, but I could tell he still felt down about it all, and that worried me. There were bound to be even more blips on the way. We'd just got started, after all, and no one ever said the homesteading life was easy. In fact, every YouTuber we watched said pretty much the opposite. But there's believing it will be hard and then experiencing the hard stuff for yourself.

Which is why I really, really hope Josh and William have a productive day today. Jack is meant to be helping them, although we'll see how that goes, and Bethany agreed to do some homeschooling with Rose.

As I come into Buckholt, I am struck by how small it is, and yet how big it feels after being in Wildflower Valley for the last few days. Its population is around four thousand according to Wikipedia, and it has one main street lined with one and two-story brick buildings, leading up to a town green with the requisite white wooden church at its far end. The library is on another side of the green, in a big brick building that also houses the town hall and courthouse.

I park outside, pay at the meter, and glance around in curiosity. It seems strange to think I'll most likely come to know Buckholt like the back of my hand, as this is where we plan to do our shopping, have our doctor and dentist visits, and anything else that requires infrastructure. Right now it looks like something out of a Norman Rockwell painting or a postcard—quaint, charming, and a little rundown.

The wind is brisk and so I don't linger, hurrying up the limestone steps to the double doors of the building. I'm just slipping inside when my phone pings with an incoming text. I finally have a signal!

The connection to the outside world feels like a literal lifeline, and I slip my phone out of my bag, eager to see the messages from my friends and family, asking how our new life in West Virginia is going.

There's precisely one text, and it's from my optician offering twenty-five percent off all prescription sunglasses valued at $250 or more.

I scroll through all my messaging apps, my stomach sinking to my toes, as I realize that no one has called, texted, messaged or tagged me since we moved. Not one person has thought to ask how we're doing.

I remind myself it's only been five days, and most people are just going about their business. Besides, they probably want to give us time to settle in. Still, it's dispiriting. One of the reasons we left New Jersey was because of the lack of connection we felt with both neighbors and friends. Life seemed too frantic to form anything meaningful; truth be told, Hooch is already a better friend to us than many of the people we knew back in Princeton. The people who didn't think to call now.

I slid my phone back into my bag, doing my best to shake off my disappointment, as I go to find a quiet space in the library where I can work.

At a desk tucked away in a corner, I set up my laptop and log into my work email. I feel a surprising sense of both comfort and energy from this, more than I usually would, back in Princeton, where logging in my hours amidst all the other stuff I had to do sometimes felt onerous.

My job is fairly boring; as a bookkeeper for a small software firm,

I basically total up columns of income and expenses, make sure they're all right, and then send out invoices and process payments. I've always liked working with numbers, especially after I had kids. I liked how dependable numbers are, compared to people. They don't cry or talk back; they don't change, and they don't contain surprises.

As I scan the first column of figures of the day, I feel something almost like relief trickle through me. I might not know the first thing about homesteading or homeschooling or any of the aspects of this new life we've chosen, but this I can do.

I work steadily all morning, occasionally checking my phone for updates from home before remembering that no one has signal so there will be no updates from family—or from anyone else, either, it seems. At lunchtime, I leave the library and walk down Main Street, looking for a place to eat.

The Mountain Grill is a classic-looking diner with deep vinyl booths and a counter in the back, with the standard cherry pie underneath a glass dome. It almost looks like a movie set, down to the waitress with the blue polyester smock and frilly apron who pours me my coffee.

I order a cheeseburger and fries and then gorge on social media while I wait for my food, catching up on everything I missed on Facebook, Instagram, and everything else, only to discover that I didn't actually miss anything, and after fifteen minutes I feel slightly sick, like I've eaten too much candy. I put my phone away as my cheeseburger comes, reminded of why we chose to homestead in the first place.

So we could get away from the life I still miss.

Halfway through my burger, my phone rings and I snatch it up like it's the holy grail. Actually, it's my father, probably the only person who really has been thinking about me and my family as we start our homesteading adventure.

"Hey, Dad," I greet him after swiping to take the call. "How are you?"

"Oh, I'm fine," my dad assures me in his gently chipper way. "The real question is, how are *you*?"

"Oh…" I let out a laugh that holds a wobble. "We're good. Getting used to a lot of things."

"I'm sure. It can't be easy."

"No, but I think we still want it to be. We've run into a few problems already, which I guess is a little discouraging."

I can be more honest with my dad than maybe I can even with Josh. I know he wouldn't chide me for being a downer, or become discouraged himself, which is what I'm afraid will happen with my husband. Besides, my dad is a great listener as well as encourager, and I know I could really use his kind-hearted whimsy right about now.

"Of course, no one wants things to be hard," my dad agrees. "But sometimes that can make it more satisfying when you manage to work out whatever it is that's a struggle. What's going on?"

Briefly I tell him about the orchard, the tiller, and even the lack of internet. "Nothing too big," I reassure him hastily, in case it sounds like I'm whining. "But I think we just feel this overwhelming need to get on top of things as quickly as we can."

"Understandable," my dad murmurs. "But it sounds like you've got things mostly under control, even if it doesn't feel like it. Do you have a plan for the trees in the orchard?"

"Just that we have to chop them down and dispose of them far away." My poor little orchard. Rest in peace.

"Why don't I come down on Saturday to give you a hand?" my

dad suggests. "I could stay for a few days and help out."

That sounds wonderful, but we also don't have room, unless my dad is up for sleeping in the unheated attic, which is currently full of boxes we haven't unpacked and probably never will. Some of the stuff from our house in New Jersey was still in the boxes we moved into it with eighteen years ago. It was easier to just move them again than go through all that stuff.

I'm about to explain this when I realize I'd really like to see my dad, and I'm pretty sure the kids and Josh would, as well. We're not *lonely* out in Wildflower Valley, not exactly, and especially not after just five days. But... a familiar face, especially my dad's kindly one, would be welcome.

"That sounds great, Dad," I tell him. "If you don't mind sharing with William..." Jack can sleep on the sofa, or in with us.

"Of course not!" my dad insists jovially. "I look forward to it. I'll see you Saturday."

After we say goodbye, I finish my burger, pay for my meal, and head back to the library for a few more hours' work. The energy I felt this morning when I logged into my work email, is already starting to dissipate. I wonder how Josh and William are making out in the meadow; is Jack helping, and did Bethany manage to teach Rose anything? I want to be there, to be part of it all, but I force myself to focus on what needs to be done.

At four o'clock, I finally clock off and head to the grocery store on the outskirts of town to pick up some supplies. I realize I am actually looking forward to this, more than my previous harried dashes around ShopRite, throwing a variety of quasi-healthy items into my cart before rushing off to do something else.

Here I go more slowly, inspecting every item, considering how to round out what we have at home, and marveling at the much cheaper prices. Eventually, we'll—hopefully, anyway—be growing our own vegetables, making our own jams, condiments, salad dressings, and even our own milk. For now, I stock up on it all, but I look forward to the day when we can say we're at least somewhat self-sufficient. Maybe even mostly, although right now, I have to admit, I throw in a box of Pop Tarts and a bag of Cheetos with gleeful abandon. We're not there yet, and I'm okay with that.

With the trunk full of groceries, it's finally time to head back to Wildflower Valley. I leave the big city behind for the rolling hills and twisting roads south, toward home. Above the dense evergreens that carpet the hills in swathes of dark green, the sky is wide open and filled with late afternoon light. Golden sunlight turns to vivid orange streaks along the horizon as I turn off Route 219 for the side road that winds down into the valley.

I drive slowly, looking around, trying to figure out where our neighbors live. On the way down to Sixpole Creek, I see a rutted dirt drive that twists through the tall trees, and I realize that must be the home of Lily and Robbie Pepper. Either that, or one of the abandoned places Hooch mentioned. It looks unlived in, save for the truck I glimpse parked in the drive, behind the trees.

At the bottom of the valley I drive across the little iron bridge that crosses the creek, now rushing wild with snow melt, and on the other side, I pass a twisting dirt road that I'm pretty sure must lead to Hooch's place. A red wooden gate swings from one rusty hinge, and I wonder how Hooch can spend so much time helping us, when it looks like his own property needs some maintenance.

I climb up a few hundred yards, the road continually twisting back on itself, and pass a neatly tended gravel driveway with a forest green five-bar gate and hand-carved wooden sign that reads 'Haven Farm'. The Hoffenbergers' place, looking as neatly tended as I'd expect, although I can't actually see their house from the road.

Finally, I'm at our own steep drive near the top of the valley. From this vantage point, it looks like the house is clinging to the steep hillside. I drive up slowly, our minivan's engine whining in protest, and then pull to a stop outside our little house.

Home.

"*Mom*!" Rose runs out onto the porch, her face smeared with jam, her expression wildly excited. It looks like little homeschooling happened today, but I tell myself that's okay.

"Hey, honey." I climb out of the car, feeling like I've been gone for an absolute age. "Can you get the others to help with the groceries?"

"Groceries…!" Rose says this like she would normally say *Christmas presents*. "Ooh, what did you get?"

"Oh, lots of stuff." I open the back of the van while Rose peers in. "What did you get up to today?"

"I memorized a poem *and* I did a math sheet," Rose states proudly. "Double digit addition!"

So some homeschooling *did* happen today. Bethany clearly cracked the whip, and I'm both impressed and gratified.

"Ooh, Cinnamon Toast Crunch!" Rose crows, holding the box aloft. All right, I caved in at Kroger. Some old habits die hard.

I grab a bag of groceries and take it inside, pausing for a moment on the doorstep to savor the fact that this is my home, and I like it. Mostly. Yes, it's still small, but the colorful afghan my mom crocheted is draped over the sofa, and the photo collage of the kids when they were all small is hanging on the wall. It really is starting to feel like home.

Jack comes careening around the corner and skids to a halt. "You're back!" He clocks the bag of groceries in my arms. "And you have food!" He stands on his tiptoes to try to peer into the bag but laughing, I dance away from him.

"Go get another bag out of the car." You'd think, I reflect as I take the groceries into the kitchen, that I starved my children.

I put down the groceries and then turn to look out the kitchen window, sending up a silent prayer that Josh and William have managed to get the Hoffenbergers' tiller working, and have tilled *something*.

A gasp escapes me at the sight of the freshly plowed meadow, its furrowed rows of dark earth touched by the last of the sun's rays, the sky streaked with vivid orange and magenta above. And yes, it looks like it's about a half-acre. I am impressed and so very grateful.

By the time we get the groceries unpacked, Josh and William are heading inside, both of them look tired and disheveled and a little dirty, but also positively triumphant. I grin at Josh.

"You did it!"

"*We* did it," Josh says, grinning back. "Took all day, and there were still some rocks we'd missed with Hooch yesterday that we had to pull out. But look out there." He turns to survey the turned-over soil from the kitchen window, his hands on his hips, very much the master of his domain.

"It looks amazing. And big!" I shake my head in wonder. I'm still nervous about maintaining that much land, but I'm determined to be enthusiastic now. "How many fence posts do you think we're going to need?"

"I did the calculations," William inserts proudly as he goes to wash his hands. "The perimeter is roughly five hundred and ninety feet, and I estimate we should have a fence post every eight feet, which comes out to 73.75 fence posts, rounded up obviously, since you can't have three-quarters of a fence post."

"Naturally," I murmur, smiling at my son. He is practically buoyant with enthusiasm.

"Plus four fence posts for corners, and another ten spares just in case one splits or rots. I estimated we'd need eighty-eight posts in total. Dad said we can head to Buckholt next week to get them."

"Make it a family trip," Josh adds as he comes to put an arm around my shoulders. "Go to the big city. How was it, anyway? How was work?"

"Good," I reply as I lean into him. "It felt strange, after being here for just a few days. But I did enjoy my cheeseburger."

"A *cheeseburger*," William groans longingly, and I laugh as I swat him on the shoulder.

"You're hardly starving! Plus I've bought plenty of goodies to see us through."

The kids start ferreting through the grocery bags, looking for snacks, while Josh and I walk out back to the plowed field.

"I know it's on a bit of a slope," he tells me, "and the Hoffenbergers insist we'll have problems with drainage, but... it's ours, and we'll be ready to plant in May."

"It's wonderful," I tell him sincerely.

"I still have to work the compost through and get the fence up. There's a lot more work to be done."

"We have time."

We are both silent as we stare out at the field. The first bright green buds are coming on the beeches and maples that skirt the meadow, and in the stillness of a sunset evening we can hear the trill of a bird—I still don't know what kind—and the burble of the creek that comes down the hillside, a cheerful sound that has grown in volume over the last few days, as the ground thaws and spring truly arrives.

"I'm sorry I was kind of grumpy and downbeat about it all for a while there," Josh tells me, shoving his hands into the pockets of his work pants. "I think I was counting on an early win, but that's not how this goes."

I let my gaze travel to the orchard with its blighted trees. "No, I guess not."

He puts his arm around my shoulders. "We'll get there. Day by day."

"Yes." I lean into him, grateful for his support. We suffered a setback, yes, but we made it through. All things considered, this feels like a win, after all.

Chapter Ten

On Friday evening, day six of our homesteading adventure, we head to the Hoffenbergers for dinner. We spent most of the day working compost into the tilled meadow, all six of us out there at one point, hoeing and raking under a surprisingly warm springtime sun while Max cantered at the edge of the field, anxious and excited in equal measure. I could have really used the internet to check on YouTube that I was doing it right, but William found some gardening books in one of the boxes we had yet to unpack, and it seems like we were, for the most part. I was trying not to second guess myself too much, but it was hard when I was constantly coming up against my own utter inexperience.

Raking through the soil was also back-breaking work. By lunchtime, all our arms were aching and by dinner we were all so filthy from tramping through the compost that every single one of us needed a shower before heading over to the Hoffenbergers. The second bathroom we are planning with the addition, I reflected, will be most welcome.

Now, as we pile into the minivan, I confess I am curious to see the Hoffenbergers' homestead. They've been at it for five years, working hard by Hooch's account, and I hope it might give us something to aim for, or at least aspire to. It's nice to be getting out all together, anyway; nearly a week into our homesteading adventure and the kids are getting a touch of cabin fever.

Last night, William and Jack were back to bickering about bedrooms and bodily functions, and Rose had a meltdown when Bethany dumped all the toys she'd set up around the room onto her bed.

"But I was *making* something," Rose wept, while I, to Bethany's chagrin, spent half an hour helping her set it all up again before tidying it up before bed.

Meanwhile Jack, who was diagnosed with ADHD just over a year ago, started getting restless, and when Jack is restless we all know it, because he gets in everyone's faces in the way he *knows* they find annoying. Josh finally came to the rescue by suggesting we all build card houses, which lasted a good half-hour before Jack purposely knocked down William's and once again fighting ensued, before William moaned, "*Why* can't we have internet?"

Yes, I think we're all ready for something a little different.

The drive down the valley road to the Hoffenbergers only takes two minutes, and then we are turning up their neatly tended driveway, going through the five-bar gate and following the lane as it curves through the forest before emerging on an open plateau. Unlike our hilly piece of land, the Hoffenbergers' is fairly flat, and I feel a twinge of envy for the stretch of verdant lawn that rolls up to a house that looks like something you'd see featured on HGTV.

"Wow," William breathes.

"Will our house look like that when it's finished?" Rose asks hopefully, and I let out a wry laugh.

"It will look a little *more* like it," I tell her.

The Hoffenbergers' house isn't that big, but compared to our semi-dilapidated ranch, it seems sprawling and massive, made of burnished pine logs with a wide wrap-around porch that sports several rocking chairs and planters filled with velvet-faced pansies and violets. As we step out of the van, I notice all the other lovely little signs of a prosperous homestead.

There's a fenced kitchen garden next to the house, with rows already coming up of what looks like early spring lettuce and spinach, and a large greenhouse to its side, its glass panes glinting in the twilight, filled with trays of seedlings and plants. Behind the house are two well-kept barns and a chicken coop with a spacious, fenced-in run; half a dozen chickens are pecking the earth and flapping their wings. In the field beyond, I glimpse the soft brown hide and big brown eyes of a Jersey cow.

Allie opens the doors and comes out onto the porch before we've even reached the steps. "Welcome, welcome," she says, her voice filled with warmth—and also pride. I can already tell she's excited to show off all that they've made here, and I can't blame her. If I were her, I'd want to show it all off, too.

Inside we all gape at the house's great room, with its massive fireplace and soaring ceiling. The staircase and upstairs hallway are open to the room, and the space is scattered with deep leather sofas and armchairs, what look like handcrafted wooden bookcases lining the walls.

"Welcome, welcome," Bill says as he strolls in from the kitchen. "We're so glad you're here."

"Would you like the tour?" Allie asks and Bill lets out a gentle laugh.

"Allie, they might want a drink first," he tells her with faint reproof. "And to sit down."

"Actually, I'd love a tour," I tell Allie. I think we're all desperately curious to see everything they've done here, and figure out how—or really, if—we can apply it to our little homestead. "What I've seen so far looks absolutely amazing."

Allie's chest swells with pride as she beams at me. "Well, we worked hard," she tells me, like a warning, and I nod, suitably chastened. This place looks like they worked *very* hard. "Why don't we start in the kitchen," she suggests, and we all follow her to a room that is the envy of anyone who has wanted a big, homey kitchen. I thought we'd allowed for plenty of space in our addition for one, but when finished it will be about half the size of the Hoffenbergers'.

I try not to feel too envious as Allie points out all the features—the deep green AGA range that takes up most of one wall, with a cast-iron stock pot bubbling away on top; the oak table that seats eight in an adjoining sunroom, the window sills filled with pots of fresh herbs; the walk-in pantry that is lined with mason jars, their contents like the colors of the rainbow—deep red beets, orange marmalade, bright yellow peaches. There's another pantry that holds sacks of flour, sugar, beans, and coffee, like something out of an old-fashioned general store. To top it all, a silky gray cat jumps off the windowsill in the sunroom where she'd been sunning herself and, tail swishing, comes over to greet us while Rose coos in delight.

"That's Misty, our mouser," Allie informs us with a chuckle. "She's friendly."

Rose is in raptures as Misty lets her pet and then even hold her, and she carries the cat around as Allie shows us the rest of the property—the wet room with double sinks and a rack of satisfyingly mud-encrusted boots; the study with two desks and a huge bulletin board full of project plans, feed schedules, and other paraphernalia of the homesteading life; the walk-in garage that has two ATV bikes, a snowmobile, and plenty of firewood.

Then we walk outside to check out the greenhouse, with its myriad seedlings and plants, the barns—one housing machinery and the other livestock—and the chicken run as well as the *other* chicken coop, behind the barns, where they keep their meat chickens.

"Best to keep them separate," Allie informs us, "since they have different feed." The poor meat chickens definitely do not get the space of the egg-laying hens, I reflect, but I guess you'd need a lot of room for that many.

Bill comes out to show us the solar panels that provide all their electricity, set up in a clearing in a nearby wood, as well as the artesian well that will still work if the power goes out. It's all incredibly inspiring, as well as a tiny bit overwhelming, because it's so *much*. It's all the plans and dreams we've had for ourselves, in living form, right here in front of us.

"It's a little like stepping into one of the Walkers' videos," Bethany whispers to me as we head back into the house, and I know exactly what she means. The Walkers are the family who got us jazzed up about the whole homesteading idea, although it originally started with Josh, who was plenty jazzed up on his own.

But the Walkers—a family with six children living in the Great Smoky Mountains of Tennessee, detailed the ups and downs of their homesteading life on YouTube, and had us all rapt, following their highs and lows. It does feel a little bit like we've walked into that realistic yet still charmed world as we survey the Hoffenbergers' homestead.

Briefly, I wonder how the Walkers are doing. We haven't watched one of their videos in weeks, and back in January, when we all went to a homesteading convention, I actually met the mother Sarah, pretty much by accident. She gave me some good advice, but she also seemed weary. Maybe that's just the nature of a busy homesteading life, but I wouldn't mind checking in with her again, although I know that's likely to be through watching one of their videos rather than a real-life chat like we had before.

Back in the house, Allie tends to whatever is still simmering on the stove, and Bill gets us all drinks—homemade lemonade or raspberry cordial, along with the blackberry wine Allie mentioned when they'd stopped over.

With drinks in hand, we all head into the great room to sit by the pleasingly crackling fire. Everything, I muse, about this place is appealing... and yet it's an awfully big house for just two retirees.

"So do you still have family back in San Francisco?" I ask Bill and then feel like maybe I shouldn't have because his kindly face droops in sadness.

"A daughter, Emily. She's twenty-seven." He hesitates like he's not sure whether he should say anymore, and then Allie comes in from the kitchen, wiping her hands on a dishrag.

"Emily stopped talking to us two years ago," she informs us in a brisk tone that I sense hides a world of pain. "She wouldn't say why. She used to come out here and seemed to enjoy it. She was supportive of our move, we wouldn't have done it otherwise..." Allie trails off as her lips tremble and then she presses them together. "Anyway. It's certainly been something of a heartache for us. She was engaged to a lovely boy, Tom, but they broke up right before she stopped talking to us. She never explained that, either." She gives a little shake of her head and then forces a smile. "Everyone's got some kind of grief, don't they? Supper's ready when you are."

We keep the conversation lighter over a delicious meal of venison stew—the deer shot and dressed by Bill himself, no less—that even Rose eats without turning up her nose, although she only recently emerged from a phase where she didn't like eating chicken nuggets because they were too "chickeny".

Allie wants to know all our plans for our homestead, and I let Josh take the lead on answering her questions because he doesn't seem to mind her constant, bossy, 'well-if-I-were-you' remarks as much as I do... although I am trying *not* to mind, because as Allie herself said, everyone's got some kind of grief, and I suspect her know-it-all busyness hides not just a loneliness, but a true sorrow. How would I feel if, ten years from now, Bethany stopped talking to me and I had no idea why? The thought gives me a great deal more sympathy and patience for Allie's commanding ways.

By the end of the evening, replete with venison stew, peach cobbler, and blackberry wine, we toddle off to our van—"you're going to need a truck in these parts!" Allie hollers after us—and back to our homestead, which does seem a little sad and small compared to the Hoffenbergers' impressive outfit.

"We'll get there," Josh says, patting my hand, as he turns off the van, and I know he's intuiting not just my thoughts, but all of ours.

"I know we will," I reply, and I mean it. Yes, there is a lot of hard work ahead of us, more than I think I can even guess at right now, and there'll be setbacks aplenty, but we *will* get there.

Right now, I feel sure of it.

Chapter Eleven

The hammering on the door starts at seven-thirty, which I suppose isn't *that* early, but we're not yet keeping country hours and so we're not up at the crack of dawn... or even at seven-thirty, as it happens.

"Hold on, hold *on*," I call as I grab a bathrobe, while Max does laps of our living room, barking, and several children emit groans from behind their own bedroom doors. Josh is still sound asleep, since he sleeps like the dead.

I open the door, thinking it might be my dad, who often wakes before the crack of dawn and might have decided to start driving here early, but it's not my father. It's a man I don't recognize, dressed in a navy-blue work jacket and pants, with a toolbelt slung around his ample hips. I'm pretty sure it's the contractor, complete with his crew, who is supposed to arrive on *Monday*, not Saturday.

"Hi..." I greet him uncertainly while he stands back and gazes up at the front of the house.

"We're here to start the work?" he tells me before calling back to someone named Jimmy to bring the tarps.

"I thought you were starting Monday—"

"An opening came up. If you want this job done, we start today." His tone invites absolutely no disagreement, and so, as Rose tiptoes into the living room in her pajamas and Max keeps barking his head off, I reply,

"That's great. Would you guys like something while you set up? Water... or coffee?"

"Cream and three sugars," the man replies without batting an eyelid. "And the boys will have the same. Four in total. Thanks."

"Great," I murmur. He's already heading back to his van.

Of course, I knew that the addition would turn our house into a building site in *theory*, but experiencing it, especially when I wasn't quite ready for it, feels like something else entirely. I'd been hoping that they would start on the side of the house, extending it to two more bedrooms and a bathroom, which would, at least in my mind, cause us the least amount of disruption, but Tony, the head guy, is insistent that they need to start in the back so they can make sure the whole site, building into the hillside as they are, is stable.

Or something like that. I didn't understand everything he said, but I got the gist, and so by nine o'clock in the morning a guy named Jimmy is marking where he's going to sledgehammer through my kitchen window eventually while the coffee I made him cools on the counter. Several other guys are outside, mapping out the foundations for the bigger kitchen.

And my dad will be here by this afternoon; it's around a six-hour drive from his condo and I'm pretty sure he would have left early.

Life, which felt so promising last night, has become instantly and overwhelmingly chaotic.

"This is a *good* thing," Josh insists as we huddle in our bedroom—the living room has become a building site even though they're not working on that room yet, with guys constantly tramping through—drinking coffee. "They're starting early."

"Two days early," I reply, "and I don't think I realized just how overwhelming it's going to be." The addition is meant to take at least four *months*. Can we really live with builders coming in and out, constant hammering and drilling and sawing, *and* the six of us relegated to our bedrooms? I feel like we did not think this through enough.

"Well, it's too late now," Josh replies cheerfully, and I have to agree with him. It's definitely too late.

Somehow, we get through the morning; the dining room off the kitchen becomes our hub of operations, with Rose doing a spelling sheet and Jack attempting pre-algebra, while William and Josh head outside to start making holes for the eighty-some posts we don't yet have.

Bethany seems restless, reading her book on herbs and then putting it down again, snapping at Rose, and then apologizing in a loop that causes me first to smile in sympathy and then grit my teeth.

"Why don't you go for a walk?" I suggest in semi-desperation when she's muttered under her breath for the fourth time that morning. "Things are starting to come up now that it's April. You could bring your book and try to identify some herbs."

Bethany stops to consider this and thankfully decides it's a good idea. She takes Max with her, and I'm just sitting down with Jack to try to remember anything about linear equations when Tony stops in the doorway of the dining room.

"We could use another round of coffee, if you're asking," he says, and I manage a smile.

"Of course," I tell him, and head to the demolition site that is now my kitchen to boil the kettle. As I stand by the sink with workmen moving around me, shouting to each other and operating various power tools, I realize that four months is far too long to simply grit my teeth and bear it.

No, I need to embrace what life is right now, in all its quite literal mess. This *is* our life for the foreseeable future, and part of the reason we chose to homestead was so we could slow down and enjoy life, rather than see it as a hassle to endure. Even if right now it feels like a hassle to endure... I don't have to let it.

And so I make the workmen coffee, accept their thanks with a smile, and head back to Jack with my own cup, when the doorbell rings. Jack bolts up from his chair; he hasn't done a single problem on his worksheet.

"Jack..." I begin, already realizing it's futile to keep him at it when someone is at the door. "Wait," I call helplessly as he races to the door and throws it open, letting out a yelp of delight.

"Grandpa!"

Chapter Twelve

When the workmen head off just after four, the blessed quiet that comes with the growl of their truck heading back down the hillside is a wondrous relief. I didn't realize just how loud they all were until they were gone... temporarily.

My dad's arrival has provided a welcome distraction, at least. He came bearing gifts—seeds for our garden, a spider plant for the house, and, best of all, pizza.

"I picked it up in Buckholt," he told me as he hefted several pizza boxes out of the back of his car. "I figure we could warm it up in the oven."

"Bless you, Dad," I told him fervently. Real pizza from a pizzeria already felt like a huge treat. I'd have been embarrassed at how pathetic that should make me feel—we couldn't rough it for so much as a week!—but I wanted the pizza too much.

Josh came in to greet my dad, and soon we were all giving him a tour of the homestead, which he's only seen in photos, stepping around workmen and speaking over the buzz of a saw as we point the barns, the plowed meadow, the blighted orchard, the pond that so far, at least, doesn't seem to have anything wrong with it, but perhaps it's just a matter of time.

Compared to the Hoffenbergers' amazing homestead, ours still felt small and kind of pathetic, but I was determined to see it at a starting point rather than a sign of some kind of failure. My dad's infectious enthusiasm helped; as we walked along, he exclaimed delightedly on just about everything, taking the problems—like the trees—in his stride. He assured us that he knew there were fast-growing fruit trees.

"You can buy them online, and they start producing fruit within a *year*. This time next year, you won't even remember those blighted trees."

I was buoyed by his attitude; it both reassured and reminded me that there are ways through the obstacles that felt like they kept getting thrown in our way. After the tour, we headed back to the house, and had the pizza for lunch, to my children's euphoria. It was only as I was handing out slices that I realized Bethany still hadn't returned from her walk, and she'd been gone for over an hour and a half.

"She's exploring," Josh said when I mentioned it, seeming unconcerned while I was already imagining her in a ditch with a broken leg or worse. "Give her her freedom.

"Okay, but in another couple of hours..."

"She'll be fine, Abby. This is why we moved."

This, and a whole lot of other reasons, but I knew what he meant, and so I let it go. We spent the afternoon in our dining room, playing cards with my dad and trying our best to ignore the racket all around us.

By four, when the workmen are leaving us in blessed quiet, Bethany still hasn't returned and now even Josh is worried.

"Where did she go?" he asks, and I nod toward the woods rising from our property, up a hillside that seems steeper and darker and more ominous, now that it's been several hours. What if Bethany fell on that rugged, rocky slope? With no cell phone signal she wouldn't have been able to call for help.

"She just started hiking up there," I tell Josh. "Past the pond. She had Max with her, though..."

Josh gives me a dubious look, because we both know that if Bethany ran into any kind of trouble, Max would be absolutely no help. He cowers when he sees a squirrel.

"She could have gotten lost," he says reflectively, scratching his cheek. "Did she have a compass?"

A *compass*? I stare at him in incredulity. Who does he think our daughter is? Do we even own a compass? And if we did, would Bethany know how to use it? Or what direction the house was in? It's not like any of us know anything about orienteering. "No, she didn't," I say, and leave it at that.

"Why don't we start looking for her?" William, overhearing our low-voiced conversation, suggests. "There are a couple of hours of daylight left. We can go in pairs."

"I'm going with Grandpa," Jack says quickly.

I hesitate, because the idea of us all up in the woods might not necessarily be a wise idea, but at the same time... Bethany has been gone for three hours. I am definitely feeling worried, and I can tell Josh is, too.

We divide into pairs—Jack and my dad, William and Josh, and me and Rose, mainly because Rose insisted she wouldn't go with anyone else. She brings Bruce along, as well, and I make a mental note to help her develop a little more resilience in this regard... another reason we moved here. It's early days for everything, I remind myself as we set off into the woods.

We each take a different direction, with Rose and I heading off west, across the hillside toward the Hoffenbergers' place half a mile away. The hill is steep, and the trees are close together, their trunks towering above us, their leaves, still just in bud, making a dark canopy above us. The ground is strewn with mossy rocks and boulders, twisted tree roots and fallen branches and brush, which make walking in a straight line nearly impossible, and our progress in general is hard going. I have to pull Rose along a little, chatting cheerfully like this is a great adventure, when in fact dread is starting to swirl in my stomach because I know my daughter, and there is no way Bethany went for a three-hour hike willingly.

Within just a few minutes, it feels like Rose and I are the last two people on earth, surrounded only by towering trees. I stop to catch my breath, straining my ears to hear the others, but the only sounds are those of the forest—the mournful call of a bird, the scolding chatter of a squirrel, and the wind soughing through the branches like a ghostly whisper.

All around us the hillside stretches endlessly, dense with trees, our little pond already vanished far below. I can't see anything but evergreen and earth, the sky seeming very high and distant above. The unease I've been feeling about Bethany uncoils like a snake in my stomach, hissing and spitting. What was I thinking, letting her go off into the woods alone?

Before we all set off, Josh gave us some tips on making sure we don't get lost in the woods—look for landmarks, find true north, and mark our trail with something memorable—a piece of twine tied around a tree, a stick stuck in the ground. It all sounded a little Boy Scoutish, but now that I'm actually alone with Rose, I appreciate the advice. Except... I didn't bring any twine, and I'm not sure how to make a memorable landmark.

And where's Bethany?

"Mom." Rose yanks on my hand. "Bruce is tired."

"And I think you're tired, too," I reply lightly. "Bruce isn't even walking."

"He's still tired," she insists, and I sigh. Now is not the time to deal with the whole Bruce thing, and how my daughter is using her teddy bear to express all her feelings.

"Okay, shall I hold him?" I ask, my voice touched with exasperation, and after a second's pause, Rose hands me her teddy bear, and I tuck him under my arm.

"Be careful," she yelps. "You're squishing him."

"He likes being cuddled." I can't believe we're talking about this. "Come on, Rose." I reach for my daughter's hand again and we keep heading up the hillside. After another five minutes of slow progress, with Rose dragging her feet, we reach a vantage point. The ground flattens out and the trees fall away, creating a small clearing of fresh green grass. Far below us I can just glimpse our house, and our little pond, glinting like a coin, tucked into the trees. Beyond the house, I see the road, snaking its way down the valley to the Hoffenbergers and Hooch's house, right by the rickety bridge over Sixpole Creek.

"What a view," I murmur, and Rose tugs my hand.

"I can't see anything."

I lift her up so she can see above the trees, and she gives a breathless giggle.

"Wow! Is that our house? It looks *tiny*."

It *is* tiny, I think as I set her down. "Pretty neat, huh?"

Rose slips her hand into mine again. "Where's Bethany?"

"I don't know," I admit, and again worry clenches my stomach.

"But we'll find her eventually, if the others haven't found her already."

"Why has she been gone so long?" Rose continues plaintively.

"I don't know," I say again. Even though the sun is warm and the air is brisk, Bethany has never been that outdoorsy a person. Why on earth would she take a three-hour walk? I can't think of a good reason other than she got lost or into trouble.

"Let's keep going," I tell Rose. "Isn't this fun? We're exploring!" I lower my voice conspiratorially. "We're going on a bear hunt. Step, step, step, I'm not scared…" I recite one of her favorite stories from when she was smaller, while Rose gives me a flat stare before pointing to Bruce.

"We already have a bear," she says.

"So we do," I reply in a normal voice. "Maybe we'll see another animal." Which is an uncomfortable reminder that when I looked up West Virginia wildlife online, I found more than I bargained for. In addition to the less alarming deer, squirrels, foxes and racoons, there are bears, bob cats, and even timber rattlesnakes, which I didn't know were a thing.

"I thought there were only rattlesnakes out west," I told Josh when I read that.

"Timber rattlesnakes?" Josh replied, frowning. "They're probably only found really deep in the woods."

His words are echoing through my head as Rose and I turn away from the clearing and head back into the deep woods, in search of my oldest daughter. What if she was bitten by a snake? Why didn't I consider such a possibility when I let her go?

I scan the ground, looking for spots where a rattlesnake might be sunbathing, fearful of treading on one half-hidden in the leaves. I think of the famous *Don't Tread on Me* flag of the Revolutionary War, which, I only learned after reading about them online, features a timber rattle snake. Clearly they don't like to be tread on.

"Mommy, I'm tired," Rose says with a huff, and I slow down for both our sakes, because I am tired, too. As we come to a step, a twig cracks underfoot, and I can't keep from jumping a little. I'm not used to being out in the wilderness, something I should have considered a little more closely when we decided to move here. I was thinking more about the lack of local amenities than this endless vista of trees and sky. And as a *vista*, it works. I like it. But when I'm in the middle of the forest and the trees are so very tall, and no matter how much I try facing north or looking for landmarks, I'm pretty sure Rose and I are lost.

I'm not so sure about all this forest now. It's so quiet, save for when I step on a stick, and while there is a beauty in the sunbeams that slant through the spaces between the towering trees, and the sheer endlessness of it is awe-inspiring, right now I want an escape route, like the side exit from a corn maze for the people who can't hack stumbling around it for more than fifteen minutes. Where is that convenient getaway now?

All I see are trees, trees, and more trees. Towering evergreens and maples and beech that block my view and whose branches obscure anything more than twenty or thirty feet ahead of us. I feel like I might as well be in the middle of the Sahara, except of course it's a forest. A *huge* forest.

Just as I'm thinking how far we are from anyone or anything—even though we've only been walking for twenty minutes—I hear the rumble of a car, faint but definite.

"I think there's a road over there," I exclaim, squinting through the trees. Have we stumbled onto civilization at last? Pulling Rose along, I hurry toward the sound, bare branches thwacking me in the face as I lurch forward.

Yes, it is a road! A cry of relief explodes out of me as we come right onto the asphalt before I pull Rose back in case another car is coming although since this is Wildflower Valley, there probably won't be another one for at least half an hour.

"Where are we?" Rose asks. There is nothing in sight but road, curving both up and down, and woods.

"We're up the road that goes by our house," I tell her, because that's the only road around here. It winds down one side of the valley, across the creek, and then up the other, and judging by the incline as well as the direction we were walking, we are near the top, above our house.

"I guess we can walk along the roadside," I say a bit dubiously, because I don't know whether we should go up or down. And what about finding Bethany?

Then, just as I am dithering about what to do, like something out of a fairytale, Bethany appears around the curve in the road, her hair tumbling down her shoulders, carrying a hemp bag that looks like it is full of flowers.

"Bethany!" Rose cries, while I simply gape.

"Where have you been?" I ask, and in my worry I sound crosser than I meant to.

"I was at Miss Barbara's," Bethany replies, like I should know who or where that is. She strolls toward us, smiling broadly. "It was *amazing*."

As she comes closer, I get a whiff of patchouli, and I remember that our neighbor who was a former yoga instructor is named Barbara. Hooch told us about her, but we haven't met her yet.

"How did you end up at Miss Barbara's?" I ask.

"Oh, I just stumbled upon her house," Bethany says airily. "Why are you guys out here on the road?"

"We were looking for you." I don't know why I feel put out. I'm relieved that Bethany is safe, and glad that she met a neighbor and seemed to have a good experience. So why do I feel... disconcerted?

"Looking for me?" Bethany arches an eyebrow as she falls into step with Rose and me and we all start walking down the winding road, toward home. "Why?"

"Bethany, you were gone for nearly *four hours*. You could have fallen and broken your leg or been bitten by a timber rattlesnake. Or both."

"Mom, come on." My daughter sounds amused. "We're not in New Jersey anymore."

Which feels like a complete non sequitur. "Yes, and you didn't go for three-hour hikes in New Jersey. Plus, there are no rattle snakes there." After learning about timber rattlesnakes, I looked it up online. They haven't been seen in New Jersey for decades.

"Ye-es," Bethany replies patiently, "but wasn't the point of moving here to give all us kids freedom and independence?"

"Ye-es," I reply right back, "but I still need to know you're safe."

Bethany's smile is strangely gentle. "That's not really freedom and independence, then, is it?" she asks.

I chew on that for a while as we walk back to the house.

Chapter Thirteen

The next morning, as I stumble from bed to feed Max and make coffee, I find my dad already up and dressed, sitting at the dining room table in a jacket and tie, dawn light streaming through the window, the freshly plowed field cloaked in an ethereal mist that rises in ghostly shreds towards a lightening sky.

"I thought we'd go to church," he says in response to my silent query.

"Oh... right." Blearily I reach for the kettle. Last night, everyone got home safely, thank goodness; Josh had made a game of it, apparently, trying to follow Bethany by noticing broken twigs and imprints in the soft dirt, like some backwoods tracker, but unfortunately he ended up following my dad and Jack's footsteps instead. They all met up at the top of the valley and walked back down just like we did, just a few minutes behind us, and everyone met back at the ranch, eager to tell their escapades, and Bethany most of all.

Apparently, she *did* get lost in the woods but then managed to battle her way through the brush and ended up stumbling upon Barbara Vesey's homestead, a tumbledown farmhouse with a wild and endless garden, at least according to Bethany.

"It was like something out of a fairy tale," she enthused, her eyes alight. "I felt like it was *enchanted*. And Miss Barbara was so friendly…"

Miss Barbara, apparently, gave Bethany fennel tea and carob and black bean brownies as well as a full tour of her extensive, wonderfully wild herb garden. *And* she offered to teach Bethany in the mystical ways—at least to me—of herbal medicine. *The Complete Herbalist* apparently lived in our midst.

"Are you sure those were *carob* brownies?" Josh asked in a hushed whisper, when we were getting ready for bed, and I had to laugh, although in truth the thought had crossed my mind, too. Bethany was so enthused about Miss Barbara; she seemed akin to a unicorn-riding princess at that point, or maybe just a funky, aging hippy, and all *that* entailed. Did I want a stranger to have so much influence *already* in my daughter's life, before I'd even met her?

I was annoyed with myself for even questioning it. Bethany was eighteen years old, and she was having fun and getting excited about what had made her want to pursue this life in the first place. I should only be grateful.

Now, as I make coffee, I consider my dad's plea for church. Growing up, I went to church every Sunday. Sunday School, youth group, the whole nine yards, but when I went off to college Sunday mornings became about sacred sleep-ins rather than dragging myself to a musty church where I didn't know anyone. Although Josh and I have taken the kids at Christmas and Easter—usually—our church attendance has never stretched to more than twice a year, if that.

And, for better or worse, we were okay with that… until we went to a homesteading convention in January, and something stirred within us. Maybe it's the connection to creation, or living more simply, but there is something holy and dare I say it, even divine about the life we are, stumblingly, trying to pursue. And so I understand why my dad is dressed in his suit and ready to head out to the nearest white-steepled house of worship, but I am also wondering if I will be able to drag four kids from their beds for such an experience.

"You all should get ready soon," my dad says meaningfully as I hand him a cup of coffee and sip my own.

"Do you know what the nearest church is?" I ask, sitting down at the dining room table to join him.

"Of course," he replies with a ready smile. "It's called Grace Church, and it's on the way to Buckholt, about five miles away."

"That's not bad," I remark. Although five miles on these back country roads when you're not a native can take a good half-hour. "What denomination is it?" At home my dad is a staunch Methodist.

"Does it matter?" he replies easily. "They preach the Good Book, and they sing hymns. That's good enough for me."

"All right," I tell him with a laugh. It could be nice to go to church, meet some near neighbors, and remember all we have to be thankful for. "What time does the service start?"

"Nine a.m. sharp."

I glance at the clock above the stove; it's just past seven. We have a little time. "I'll wake everybody at eight," I promise my dad. "It's a good idea."

He smiles at me, his expression softening. "Your mother would be glad you think so."

I smile back, but with a pang in my heart because even though my mom died over four years ago now, at times like this it can still feel fresh. She was funny and almost painfully pragmatic, with a briskness that was too cheerful ever to be callous, but boy, did she tell you like it was. I still miss her and think of her every day.

"What do you think Mom would think of us moving out here?" I ask my dad. "Really?"

He frowns in thought, his shaggy eyebrows drawing together as he considers his answer. "I think she would consider you crazy and brave in just about equal measure. And she'd be envious and tell you so, because she'd always wanted to do the same thing."

I laugh, because I know he's right, but my laugh ends on a sigh that could easily turn into a sob. Somehow, in my old suburban life, when each day marched on the same, I didn't have to think about my mom too much, except in vulnerable moments, when I felt tired or lonely.

But here... when so much is new and exciting and scary and hard? I wish she was here to give me her advice, to roll up her sleeves and work right alongside me, to briskly inform me that I had my work cut out for me, *that* was for sure, and she hoped I wouldn't regret it.

"I know," my dad says, though I haven't said anything. He pats my hand as he gives me a smile that holds so much sorrow. "I miss her, too."

I nod, a lump forming in my throat, and then Jack stumbles out of the bedroom, groaning about how he is definitely not the one who snores, and is there any more Cinnamon Toast Crunch for breakfast.

"Considering I bought the box two days ago," I tell him, "there'd better be."

There isn't. Two telltale bowls in the sink with a single dried-out cinnamon square are testament to someone's late night snack. I sigh and then tell Jack he can have bacon and eggs for breakfast, which is much better, anyway.

I start cracking eggs into a bowl, moving around the drop cloths and stepladders the workmen left, taking a little of my mom's cheerful briskness for my own. Outside the sky is still pink at the edges, and a pale, pearly blue high above. A robin—I recognize that bird, at least—alights on a branch outside the window that is just beginning to bud, tightly furled cherry blossoms that I know will unfurl into giant pink puffballs in a week or two. The world is waking up, and our adventure has more than begun.

In a couple of weeks, we can start to plant, and get our first chicks, and who knows what else. Growing a garden and getting chickens were at the top of our lists because every seasoned homesteader said those were the gateway into the whole lifestyle, and right now they feel just about manageable... as does going to church.

We arrive at Grace Church five minutes late, pulling into a gravel parking lot filled with pickup trucks. We have to park on the grass and then tiptoe in and cram ourselves into the last pew while the band at the front strikes up a bluegrass version of *Amazing Grace*.

Surprisingly—or not—none of my children put up a fight about going to church. Maybe, like me, they sense the presence of something greater than themselves in the towering trees, the rushing streams, the Appalachian Mountains that rise in endless, rolling tree-covered peaks on the horizon.

As we squeeze into the pew, I look around at the congregation—mostly families, all in their Sunday best, which ranges from pressed jeans and flannel shirts to dresses in floral or paisley patterns. As we reach for our hymnals, a little girl with bright blond braids and a face full of freckles turns around to gaze at us unabashedly, and then sticks her tongue out at Jack, who, I am sorry to say, sticks his tongue out right back at her, and puts his fingers in his ears.

I bat his hands away from his ears just as the girl's mother turns around and, in the way that only mothers can, gives the girl a friendly but warning swat. Clearly she knows her daughter very well or has eyes in the back of her head or both, because I'm pretty sure nothing about that little exchange passed her by.

She glances from Jack to me, her look both friendly and considering, and after a second's pause I find a smile, and then she smiles and nods back. She looks to be in her forties, with the capable air of a countrywoman, dressed in what looks like a hand-knit sweater in a bright patchwork pattern and a long, flowing denim skirt. She turns around again, and I find my page in the hymnal and start singing.

The service passes in a flow of song, prayer, and a heartfelt sermon where the preacher raises his voice so he's practically shouting, Southern style. The kids are a little taken aback by his vigorous manner, but I think after that first shock—a booming 'Can I get an Amen?'—they start to enjoy it, and I do, too.

If I had in my head that we might make a semi-quick getaway afterward, though, I am soon to be disappointed. As soon as the blessing is pronounced, we are besieged.

It's almost like everyone timed it—they surge toward us in unison, a vast army in denim and flannel, floral and plaid, coming for us. Rose inches closer to me. Jack looks awed. Even Josh's ever-present smile slips a little.

A rotund woman with a head of frizzy gray hair gets to us first.

"So you must be that city family that bought Jethro's old place," she announces to what feels like the entire congregation. "From New Jersey or some such, did I hear that correctly? And your name is Bryant?" I open my mouth to reply in the affirmative, but she steamrolls over me. "You broke your tiller, didn't you, and you've got fire blight in your orchard. Terrible thing, that. My Ralph will come over with his log splitter if you need it. You've got to get those trees out, mind, and fast."

"Um... thank you," I say, feeling inadequate to this whole conversation. "Yes, we didn't realize about the blight..."

The woman clucks her tongue in what feels like kindly censure. What kind of greenhorn, that cluck says, doesn't get their trees checked out before buying a woodland property? Well, obviously this one.

"Anyway," she says, squeezing my arm, "we've all been wondering about you. There's been plenty of people who've come this way and bought up some land and thought they could make a go of it." She pauses, her lips pressing together. "Well, they couldn't."

"So we've heard," I reply, trying for a light tone. "I hope we'll be different."

"Well, you've got the good Lord on your side," the woman replies, squeezing my arm again. "And surely more common sense than to come up here with your camper van, stick some seeds in the ground and call it a day." She shakes her head in derision, and I am not about to point out that change camper to mini and we've more or less done the same thing. Over the last few days I've been feeling less out of my depth, but that sense of inadequacy is coming back with a vengeance, and that's thanks to—what I suspect this woman thinks—is her *encouraging* me.

"What did you say your name was?"

"Oh, bless you, honey, I don't think I ever did! I'm Patricia Leroy, but everyone calls me Miss Patti. Now." She turns to look expectantly at my brood, all of whom have been skulking behind me while Josh heads off for a conversation with Mr. Leroy. "Who are all these lovely folk?"

I duly introduce all my children, and they more or less mumble their greetings.

Miss Patti's eyes narrow as Bethany, at least, manages to speak up a little.

"Well…" she says in reply, drawing out the syllable, and I can tell she is unimpressed by their performance.

"And this is my dad," I say a little desperately, "Will Carson."

"A pleasure to meet you," my father booms in a rich baritone that he doesn't usually employ, and Miss Patti smiles, satisfied.

There is a line of at least a dozen people waiting to talk to us, and I already feel limp with exhaustion.

Somehow, we get through a good half-hour of pleasantries. I lose count of the number of times I have to explain how we didn't know about the fire blight, when it seems like everyone else in the entire county did. I field questions that are alarming in their knowledgeable nature—people I've never set eyes on before know we have a dog named Max, we broke our tiller on the first day, we're 'doing something fancy' to the house, and I've driven to Buckholt to work in the library.

By the time the last person gives a cautionary cluck—a sound I have heard too many times already—my head is spinning.

"Lord, you must be exhausted," a woman exclaims, and I turn to see the woman who smiled at me during the service standing in front of me. She's got a baby on her hip and a toddler hiding behind her skirts, and at least three other children with the same straw-colored hair standing near her. "I'm Emmy Wilson," she tells me, balancing the baby so she can hold out a hand for me to shake. "We live about three miles past Wildflower, in the next holler."

"Holler?" I repeat uncertainly, distantly recalling that Hooch had used the same word, and she laughs, a clear sound that rings like a bell through the church.

"Hereabouts we call a valley a holler. Wildflower Valley is called what it is on the map, maybe, but everyone who knows calls it a holler."

"Wildflower Holler," I repeat slowly. It doesn't, I confess, have quite the same ring.

"You'll get the way of it eventually," Emmy replies. "If you decide to stay."

"Oh, we're staying," I say firmly, because after half an hour of local chitchat, I'm getting fed up with people assuming, nicely enough, that we won't.

Emmy nods approvingly. "That's the spirit. Well, if you get tired of it all and you need a break, come round to my place for a cup of coffee or something stronger. Bring the kids, or if you'd rather, don't." She laughs again, loud and clear. "It's on the road to Buckholt, three miles out of Wildflower. There's no number but it's got a red gate and an old watering can with flowers in it by the road. Come anytime. I'm almost always in." She reaches out to grasp my hand again, her grip firm and sure, and I murmur something grateful in reply.

As we step out into the spring sunshine, I wonder if I might have made a friend.

Chapter Fourteen

On Monday morning, the workmen return with their hammering and tramping through the house and seemingly endless requests for coffee, and after filling them for a second time, we all escape to Buckholt, leaving poor Max contained in the dining room, looking miserable to be left alone. My dad is still here, seeming unfazed by all the chaos, and we're on a mission to buy eighty-four fence posts and maybe even look at some chicks.

"I hope they deliver," I tell Josh as we drive out of the valley, or rather, the holler. Since we live in West Virginia, we should probably start using the West Virginian terminology, but it doesn't come naturally. Not yet, anyway.

"Well, about that..." Josh says with the kind of sheepish grin I know well.

"About eighty-four posts?" I ask, my voice sharp with suspicion.

"I figured we really need a truck," my husband states baldly. "I mean, who homesteads with a minivan?"

There's some truth to that, but I can tell by the way he says it that he expects me to resist, which is perfectly understandable because when it comes to our marriage, that's pretty much been my job.

But right now, I don't want to be the one who errs on the side of caution, who tells everyone to slow down, be sensible, don't go crazy. Right now I just want to get on board and be excited.

"Okay," I say, and it feels like everyone in the minivan, my dad included, does a doubletake. "Let's get a truck. I'm assuming you've looked up a dealer in Buckholt?"

Josh's grin turns even more sheepish. "Well, I might have, when I got signal on my phone when we were searching for Bethany."

"Ah, of course." I mock-slap my forehead. "And so?"

"Mom," Bethany asks suddenly. "Are you okay?"

I laugh. "Yeah, I'm fine," I assure her. "But clearly we need a truck."

She shakes her head slowly. "Why aren't you telling Dad that we can make do with the minivan for a few more months, until we find our feet, make sure of what we need, that we've stayed in our budget..." Unconsciously or not, she's adopted my lecturing tone, and that makes me both grimace and chuckle.

"Because if we're going to pick up eighty-four fence posts today, we need a truck. And anyway, the minivan was only a temporary solution. I don't see us getting up our driveway in the dead of winter in that thing."

Everyone is silent for a moment, and then Rose pipes up, "Can I get a cat today?"

"And I can get a gun?" Jack asks.

Clearly they're sensing a soft touch. "No," I tell my children, turning around to smile at them all, as well as my dad, who is looking, as usual, cheerfully benevolent. "I think we'll stick with just a truck." I pause. "And maybe some chicks."

"Chicks!" Rose exclaims. "Really, we can get chicks *today*?"

"Well..." Besides a broken-down old chicken coop, we do not currently have all the things we need to nurture baby chicks—a brooder, a heat lamp, bedding, starter feed... I *have* done my research there, at least, and I know that everyone says chickens are the easiest animal to start with. So, if not today, then when? "Yes," I tell Rose and the others, my voice firm. "Assuming the feed store has them, we can get them today."

An hour later, we're driving down Buckholt's Main Street, slow enough that we can check out all the stores—the diner where I ate lunch, a consignment store, a bakery, a health food place, a women's clothing boutique, a pharmacy. They're all independent and look impossibly quaint as well as a little rundown—no massive RiteAid or Whole Foods here, something I appreciate, even if I still miss the convenience of such places.

Everyone is quiet, and I wonder what they are thinking. This now, is our booming metropolis. It's both inspiring and a little nerve-wracking.

"Can we park and walk around?" Bethany asks.

"Sure... why don't I drop you all off," Josh suggests, "and then I'll go check out the truck."

"The truck," I repeat with a knowing nod. "So you already have a particular one in mind?"

"Yep." Josh doesn't bother to look sheepish this time. "A 2004 Ford Ranger with one hundred and twenty thousand miles on it. It's only three thousand bucks. I figure we'd go with a jalopy until we found our feet."

"Dad, did you just say *jalopy*?" Bethany asks incredulously. "That word was on my SATs."

"Who says I don't have an excellent vocabulary?" Josh asks, grinning back at Bethany.

"I don't think anyone said that," I murmur. "But it makes more sense to drive to the dealership and drop *you* off. Then you can meet us back in town in your new jalopy."

"Is that an oxymoron?" William muses. No one answers, probably because excellent vocabulary or not, none of us is sure.

Soon enough, we've dropped Josh off and I'm driving us all back into town. We park by the green, just as I did before when I went to the library and then start strolling into town. It's a sunny spring day—blue-skied, with a breeze that is definitely a little on the chilly side, but the cherry blossoms are coming out, and the day feels full of promise. Rose holds my hand as she skips along, and Bethany stops to study some notices in the window of the health food store.

"Miss Barbara mentioned this place," she tells me. "Apparently they have some great essential oils."

I don't think my daughter used an essential oil once in her life before she packed in her schooling and decided she wanted a career in herbalism, if such a thing even exists. But I tell myself that's fine; everybody gets to decide who they are and what they're interested in, and more importantly, they're allowed to change their mind about those things, too. And, as I know Bethany herself would remind me, this kind of thing was the reason, or one of them, that we moved here.

We spend a good hour exploring Buckholt, ducking in and out of various stores that are quaint but also a little bit rundown, which is, really, the vibe of the whole town. Charming but has seen better times, but then, haven't we all? This part of central West Virginia is clearly a mix of experienced locals and homesteaders or retirees like us and the Hoffenbergers, who come in with money and a lot of optimism. With nearly every store we go into, I can tell the sales assistant has known immediately which category to put us into.

We are just considering our lunch options—the diner or Mamma Mia, an Italian eatery that has a preponderance of fake greenery around its front door—when Josh pulls up in what else but a battered yet impressive 2004 Ford Ranger, his elbow resting on the open window.

"Howdy, strangers," he greets us in a wide West Virginian drawl, and Bethany briefly closes her eyes.

"Dad, don't ever do that again," she says, but Jack and William are already running up to the truck, William running his hand along its side the way you might a horse, if he liked either horses or trucks, which he never has before. I guess we're all allowed to change.

"Pretty sweet, huh?" Josh exclaims to William and Jack. He still has the trace of a West Virginian drawl, but I don't think he even realizes.

"Yeah, totally," William says. "Can we get the fence posts now?"

"What about lunch—" This from me.

"We'll get something on the way over there," Josh says with a wave of his hand. "Dinah's Home Cookin' is on the way and they do all-day biscuits and gravy."

I'm not sure any of my children have had biscuits and gravy; none of us are connoisseurs of Southern cooking, but everyone seems to want to head out to the feed store—the girls for chicks, the boys for fence posts—so we pile into the minivan, with William and Jack going with Josh in the truck, and then we leave the delights of Buckholt behind for Dinah's Home Cookin'—Josh insists everyone tries the biscuits and gravy, and everyone likes them, even Rose—and then the feed store, a sprawling building with a huge sign out front advertising manure by the cubic yard.

"If we had a milk cow," William informs me as we pull into the parking lot, "we wouldn't need to buy manure."

"That is very true," I tell him. Apparently, in addition to compost, we should be working manure through our freshly tilled soil. I'm not sure we should be getting a cow just for its manure, but who knows, maybe that's a thing. The milk might just be a bonus.

In addition to the sign for manure out front, there is one proclaiming: IT'S SPRING! TIME TO HATCH! Which I assumed meant we could expect some chicks.

The feed store is as big as a Target—not that I'm wistful—but it smells like a cross between a pet store and a barn, which, to this ex-suburbanite, is not the most pleasant of aromas. Still, I'm determined to be game. While Josh, William, Jack, and my dad go to check out the fence posts, Bethany, Rose and I go in search of chicks. We're directed to what is basically a massive cage in the center of the store, about the size of a pickleball court, not that I ever played. Plenty of my friends did though.

It contains several long, narrow metal tubs with heat lamps positioned for the baby chicks, which are blundering about in the tubs, woodchips stuck to their fuzz as they chirp and squawk.

"*Oh!*" Rose exclaims, already enraptured.

Bethany peers into one tub. "Okay, they are actually cute," she says.

A member of staff lets us into the cage as she cheerfully informs us that we're lucky there are any chicks here at all. Thanks to the avian flu, chicks—as well as chickens and their eggs—have become unbelievably scarce.

"We've got Rhode Island Reds and Speckled Sussex," she tells us, "and not much else. You're lucky there was a delivery today—these little guys are snapped up almost as soon as they arrive."

"Mommy, we have to get them," Rose implores, her hands clasped to her chest like she's an extra in *Oliver!*. "Please..."

"How much are they?" I ask the lady who let us into the cage.

"The Speckled Sussex are two ninety-nine a chick," she informs. "The Rhode Island Reds are three-fifty."

They *are* cute, I think as I stoop over one of the tubs. They're little puffballs, all fuzz and eyes with a tiny beak. They look like something out of Pokémon.

"We're first-time hen owners," I tell the woman baldly, accepting that I'm likely to be fleeced. "How many would you suggest we buy?"

"How big a chicken run do you have?"

"Non-existent at the moment," I reply. "We have a rundown coop and space for a run outside that might be..." I glance at Bethany, as if she's already done the calculations, and she frowns.

"Ten by twenty?" At best it's a guess.

"From the sounds of it," the woman tells us with a slow nod, "I think you should start with six."

For some reason, I feel disappointed. I think of the Walker family on YouTube with their forty meat chickens and another dozen egg-laying hens, and six measly chicks feels like a failure.

"We'll take eight," I say firmly. Rose beams delightedly and Bethany looks impressed.

"We're really doing this?" she asks, and I nod.

"We are."

Fifteen minutes, we have a cardboard box scattered with woodchips and eight little puffball chicks nosing around its confines. They're "unsexed", meaning we can't yet tell if we've got roosters or egg-laying hens, which feels like a pretty big gamble, but apparently that's how it's done. We'll know soon enough, the woman tells me with a laugh.

I add some chick starter feed and an infrared heat lamp to our order as well as a container for water, and amazingly, we're good to go. That's all we need to start, and the chicks will be staying inside with us until they're five weeks old and fully feathered, so we have a little time to build the chicken run.

While I pay for everything, Rose jumping up and down in excitement beside me, Bethany goes to find the boys.

"They're loading the fenceposts into the truck," she tells me when she returns. "So it looks like we're all ready."

Soon enough, we've got all we came for, and we're piling back into our cars for the ride home.

Home. I glance at the box of chicks on the seat next to Rose—the boys all went in the truck—and I feel a little leap of excitement in my chest. We've taken so many steps today, and it feels good. Right.

"You should probably get some milk, while we're here," Bethany remarks as we pass Kroger on the way back into Buckholt.

"You're right. You guys stay in the car with the chicks. I'll be quick."

As I hurry into the store to buy some much-needed milk, I wonder if maybe we should get a dairy cow sooner rather than later.

Chapter Fifteen

Over the next three weeks, spring comes to Wildflower Valley—or Holler—in a riot of color. The steep slopes that were brown and bare are now lush with grass and dotted with wildflowers—Virginia bluebells, white trilliums, pink and purple anemones, and yellow lady's slipper all tangled up together among the long green grass, bright heads tilted toward the sky.

Bethany brought a book on local wildflowers back from Miss Barbara's and Rose and I take several nature walks through the hills—I bill them as school field trips, which they *are*—and identified all the ones we could, much to her delight. Spring here feels sweeter than back in New Jersey, although admittedly it was beautiful there too, and a small part of me still misses the manicured gardens and endless cherry trees we used to see in Princeton.

But here in the rolling hills of central West Virginia, the air is fresh and the mornings sparkle with dew; there is wildlife *everywhere*, from the deer that edge out from the woods, their delicate heads bent to the soft, fresh grass, to the fat raccoon that lumbers up a tree, its backside waddling comically. Red-breasted robins flit between budding trees, along with a few other birds I've come to recognize, thanks to another book from Miss Barbara.

From the kitchen window I point them out to Jack, who, with

the help of my dad's binoculars, which he left after he went back to Bucks County after a wonderful week, has taken a surprising interest in birdwatching. We see yellow and black goldfinches and bright red Northern cardinals; vivid bluejays and more muted sparrows and nuthatches. Jack exultantly identifies a red-bellied woodpecker in the maple tree by the barn, and more than once we glimpse a red-shouldered hawk soaring high above our homestead, its elegant wings outstretched. Looking up at the fearsome bird of prey, I'm glad our chicks are still safe inside.

Of course, life isn't a *Snow White*-esque montage where we're singing to the squirrels and letting bluebirds perch on our fingertips. Amidst the beauty of the wild world around us, there's a lot of hard work to be done. It takes Josh, William, Jack and my dad two full days to get all the fence posts in, and then another day to mix and pour the concrete around each one, and *then* a further two days to attach the wire and rails to each hard-fought post. By the end of the week, however, we have a fenced-in vegetable patch, and it looks good. Mostly, anyway.

"The next time we do that," Josh tells me, his hands planted on his hips in a satisfied manner, "it will be a lot faster."

Considering how long this effort took, I hope the next time isn't anytime soon.

While Josh and the boys have been working on the fence, along with my dad, Bethany has been spending a lot of time up at Miss Barbara's, and I've been trying to homeschool Rose—and Jack when I can catch him—and taking care of our baby chicks as well as planning the layout of our vegetable garden, and also squeezing in my twenty hours of work in Buckholt.

Rose takes great interest in the three-hundred-page seed catalogue

I picked up at the feed store, and we scrap her reading primer for paragraphs on heirloom tomatoes and rainbow carrots, laboriously studying description of every vegetable variety and debating the merits of quick-growing and hardy plants versus plentiful and prone to pests.

Meanwhile, the workmen move all around us, sawing and hammering, and asking for coffee refills every few hours. I've come to know them, in a roundabout way, and I ask Bob about his kids and Ray about his fiancée, and in between chats while the kettle boils, the foundation and frame of our kitchen addition goes up. I am starting to envision what my beautiful, big kitchen will look like in a few months, with a big butcher block island in the center and a six-burner stove along one wall, a window seat overlooking the backyard and a big, farmhouse kitchen sink. I can hardly wait.

But just in case our life sounds like the opening credits to *Little House on the Prairie*, one long, blissed-out montage of bucolic moments, it's not. There are plenty of hassles and heartaches along the way, with Rose having a tantrum every other day about math and Jack hitting William's thumb with the hammer not once but *twice*—by accident, at least, not that that made much difference to poor William and his thumb. We debated a visit to the ER in Buckholt, but even William decided he didn't want to make the drive. In due course, his thumbnail turned black and fell off and Rose said it was basically a science experiment. I thought about having her write a lab report, but that seemed like a step too far.

One night, three weeks after our move, Bethany has a mini meltdown, burying her head in her arms at the dining room table as she moans that maybe she should have applied to college after all, and what on earth was she meant to do with her life out here in the sticks?

I resist any I-told-you-so-response that she accuses me of anyway, tearfully reminding me that she was *allowed* her emotions, and to be fair, there was probably a hint of told-you-so-ness in my tone, as much as I tried to keep myself from it.

And beyond all those child-related woes, which come in every season of parenthood, we're trying to be frugal—at least *I* am, Josh admittedly less so—but we still seem to spend money like water; the kitchen alone is costing nearly twice as much as we'd initially thought, for reasons I don't entirely understand, but have to do with the rocky soil and disrupted supply chains. Considering the semi-finished state of our house, what can we do but write another check?

And besides the renovation, life in Wildflower Valley isn't so very self-sustaining, at least not yet. Josh drives out to Buckholt at least twice a week, claiming, most likely reasonably, that he needs something—another tool or bag of compost or *something*. And, full disclosure, I do the same. When I head into town for work, I often end up picking up a packet of seeds or a new gardening fork or even just something easy from Kroger for dinner. I'm not in full homesteading make-everything-from-scratch *just* yet, not by a long shot.

But even that feels like something we expected and can deal with. We put enough cushion in our budget that the alarm bells don't need to be ringing yet. And yet... in my quieter moments, when busyness overtakes me, other alarm bells are.

Because the truth is, in the midst of all the serene beauty of a West Virginia springtime, I find myself missing things I didn't expect to—traffic and streetlights and texts from my friends. Netflix, even though I almost always fell asleep in the middle or even the beginning of whatever we were watching . Friday night take-out, ordered with ease on a phone. Browsing the newspaper for events to consider going to that we usually never did. There was so much *possibility* in our old lives, even if we rarely took advantage of it. It was still *there*.

Here there is a different kind of possibility, one that is wrapped in mundanity. As all the YouTubers warned us, homesteading is a lot of work. A lot of boring, backbreaking work, day after day after day. We haven't even planted our vegetable garden yet, and weeds are already coming up, pushing defiantly through the damp earth. The chicks, although tiny, still take a lot of care, or at least more than I expected, as well as a significant portion of our dining room, which, thanks to the renovation, is our main living space. Building the fence alone took over a week, and we still have to work more compost through the soil; we have two more *tons* of it being delivered next week.

And then there is a list of jobs on the fridge that just seems to get longer—deal with the blighted trees, comb the property for dead trees for firewood, hauling them back and chopping them up without the benefit of a log splitter, start tomatoes and cucumbers inside, chit potatoes, fix the chicken coop and build a chicken run ... and that's just for a start.

The more we do, I know, the more jobs there will be, and I know that's the point, that we entered into this life *so* we could do these things. This list of jobs isn't, the way it so often is in suburban life, something to be endured so we can move on to do something else more interesting or important. These jobs *are* our lives, or at least the main part of each and every day. If I can't enjoy them, what am I even doing here?

These kinds of thoughts put me in danger of having some kind of existential crisis, and so I try not to think about them too much.

There's a lot to do, after all, and I could push it all to the back of my mind if I tried hard enough, but... one night toward the end of April, when we are getting ready to plant and the workmen's hammering has been endless, we're meant to be putting our chicks into the coop which isn't ready yet, despite William and Josh's best efforts at making an enclosed chicken run, I cave and give in to a little existential angst.

"Do you think we did the right thing, in moving here?" I ask Josh as we climb into bed, keeping my voice low so that the kids can't hear. The walls, I know, are pretty thin.

He cocks an eyebrow at me, deliberately unperturbed. "What's brought this on?"

"I know we did it and we're here and we have to make the best of it," I say in a rush. "I'm not arguing any of that. It's just... were we crazy? I mean, maybe we should have just binge-watched *The Waltons* or *Little House on the Prairie* for a couple of weeks. Got it out of our system rather than leave everyone and everything we've ever known."

"Abby." Josh's voice is kind, but with the teensiest note of impatience. This, for him, is old ground, already well and truly covered. "This was bigger than that. It wasn't some *whim*. We spent a year deciding to do this."

"You mean," I reply, half-teasing, half-serious, "you spent a year trying to convince me."

"And I thought I did." He rests his head back against the pillows as he gazes at me seriously. "Why the second thoughts now? Getting to the root of that is probably more helpful than revisiting a decision we made some time ago and would be pretty hard to unravel at this point, not that you're suggesting we do that." He speaks levelly, but

I sense his frustration. We really should have moved past this kind of self-doubt. *I* should have, and I thought I did. I suppose it shouldn't come as a huge surprise that I'm circling back to it.

We've been in West Virginia for almost a month, and the newness of it has, perversely, gotten old. I'm tired of not knowing where things are, of not having friends, of needing to find new doctors and dentists and make all the requisite appointments. I'm tired of life being different and strange and hard.

But beyond that... and this is where the existential angst hits home, I don't know if I am going to *like* this life, when I think about it in the long term. Will planting a garden and canning tomatoes really satisfy some restless part of me? Do I want to homeschool Rose for the next twelve years? Do I want to live in a place where I can count my neighbors on one hand, as kind as they've been? Hooch has stopped by at least twice a week, and he's always willing to jump in and help William and Josh with whatever they're doing. Allie Hoffenberger came by with some early lettuce, but also, I'm pretty sure, to inspect the progress of our addition. Still, it was kind of her, and I promised we'd invite them over when we had a complete kitchen.

But beyond that... what about our kids? Will *they* like it here, for the rest of their lives at home? A month in, and I'm worried they are experiencing the same kind of restlessness I am. Back in New Jersey, Jack would be starting baseball. William would be entering chess tournaments. Bethany would be shopping for her prom dress.

The other morning, I came into the kitchen to see William playing chess by himself. I valiantly offered to play him, and he just gave me a pitying look. "Mom, I can beat you in under a minute."

"Maybe we can find someone here to play," I suggested. "A chess club in Buckholt...?"

"There isn't one." He moved a piece on the board. "It's fine."

But was it fine? Was this kind of isolation really good for children? For *me*?

"Abby?" Josh prompts.

I already know I can't articulate my own uncertainty to my husband; telling him now that I'm not sure homesteading is my thing would be both discouraging and pointless—for both of us. It has, after all, only been a month, and a challenging one at that, with our home a building site. I have to give this life a chance... but right now I also have to tell Josh something.

"I'm worried about the kids," I blurt. "We've been here a month, and they haven't made any friends. There aren't any friends to *make*."

Josh frowns thoughtfully. "There's a homeschool co-op in Buckholt..."

"An hour away?" I protest skeptically. "And I'm not sure that's enough."

His frown deepens as he considers this dilemma. "Remember that child psychologist who said friends were overrated for children? How it's much more important to have a stable family life?"

"*Ye-es*, but they need *some* friends, Josh. Some outlets." And so, I realize, do I.

Josh is silent for a moment, thinking. "We knew this would be an issue going in," he reminds me, like that matters now.

"Yes, and it's one we need to figure out." A sigh escapes me, a sound of regret that Josh notices, and his jaw tenses. "I guess I hoped there would be more kids locally," I admit. "If not in Wildflower Valley, then nearby." I'd been imagining, I realize, a family like the

Walkers, of YouTube homesteaders' fame. A family like us, who lived in the city but chose the country, and straddled both worlds in a way that felt relatable.

"Maybe we should go back to that church," Josh remarks. We haven't been back since my dad was here, nearly three weeks ago now, and next Sunday is Easter. "There were plenty of kids there. And what about that woman you talked to? Didn't you say she invited you over?"

"Well, theoretically," I reply, recalling Emmy Wilson's ready smile and firm handshake. I've been meaning to stop by as she asked, but somehow it felt presumptuous and there wasn't enough time anyway. "We didn't fix a date or anything."

"So?" Josh arches an eyebrow in challenge. "You know what you'd say to the kids in this situation, right?"

I roll my eyes good-naturedly, managing a smile. "I'd tell them they need to get out there and make an effort, that you can't make a friend while sitting in your house." Or some bracing variation thereof.

"Exactly. Why don't you take the kids with you? That family looked like they had some kids that matched ours in age."

"Bethany and William will *not* go for that," I warn him. "Because it will be, you know, *awkward*." Which I have long ago learned that for teenagers, is worse than death.

"They might surprise you," Josh says seriously. "They've changed since they've been here, Abs. I know it's only been a month, but William has so much more confidence—he sunk the last twenty posts in by himself. And Jack is raring to go, up for anything... plus Bethany's already made a friend, even if she's sixty-seven years old."

Which reminds me that I really need to walk up the hill and meet the famous Miss Barbara.

"Give them a chance," he urges me, but what it really feels like he's saying is to give myself a chance. Because while the kids might have changed, right now I'm wondering if I have—or will.

Chapter Sixteen

Emmy Wilson's driveway is just as she described—three miles away from Wildflower, in the next holler, with a red wooden gate and a rusted watering can that has a few yellow tulips poking out. It's a couple days after my bedtime chat with Josh, and I've corralled the kids in the car and brought them all over to meet the Wilsons. To my surprise, they were all amenable, to varying degrees—Rose was eager, Jack cautiously optimistic, William wary, and Bethany pragmatic.

"I mean, I know we need to meet people here," she said with an accepting shrug. "How many kids do they have?"

"I don't actually know," I admitted. "Quite a few."

Now, as I drive through the gate and up a drive that's nearly as steep as hours, I can't keep a certain social anxiety from making me grip the steering wheel a little too tightly. Cold-calling a neighbor is something I haven't done for a very long time. What if Emmy Wilson didn't actually *mean* the invitation? I can't count all the times back in New Jersey I'd run into someone at the post office or grocery store, and we'd effuse over seeing each other again and make deliberately vague promises of getting together, safe in the knowledge that we never would.

Was Emmy's invitation the West Virginia version of that? Maybe

I should have realized she didn't mean to *actually* come over, and certainly not with all four kids. Yet here we are.

As I reach the top of the hill, the Wilson farmhouse comes into view. It's made of weathered white clapboard, with a few shutters askew and a sagging front porch that is full of planters, rocking chairs, and rusty bikes. There are two old pickup trucks parked in front, one up on concrete blocks, and a red wooden barn looms behind the house, where a few scraggly-looking chickens peck at the dirt.

The whole place has the air of being lived in, maybe a little too much. It's not a patch on the Hoffenbergers' palace of a place, where everything is so new-looking and neatly kept, and yet there is something shabbily lovable and real about it all. As I put the car into park, a dog sets to barking and the grimy face of a child appears in the front window before disappearing again.

"Well." I let out a breath. "Here we are."

Nobody moves. Now that we're at the Wilsons' house, I'm pretty sure we're all in the grip of some serious social anxiety, and I know I need to be the one to lead the way.

"Let's go!" I call cheerily, and then I open the car door. Slowly my children unbuckle their seatbelts and climb out, all four of them looking deeply reluctant as we make our way to the sagging front porch.

"Well, look what the cat dragged in!" Emmy calls merrily as she opens the door. She's wearing a blue gingham dress that looks like something Mrs. Walton would put on to do the laundry, paired with a fisherman knit cardigan that hangs nearly to her knees. Her straw-colored hair, streaked with silver, is scooped up in a messy bun, and not the artful kind. There is something very *real* about Emmy

Wilson that makes me warm to her instantly and instinctively. I find myself smiling.

"I'm sorry I didn't come before," I tell her as she waves us all into a cluttered hallway that is dark and shabby, full of coats and boots. I step over a cat litter box that has been crammed into one corner and looks well-used. I open my mouth to say some excuse—because that's exactly what it would be—and then stop. I already feel with Emmy Wilson that no excuse is necessary.

"The important thing is you came now," Emmy says, taking my arm and drawing me into the kitchen which is just as cluttered and chaotic as the hall, and, I suspect, the rest of the house. There is stuff everywhere—and not in an aesthetic way, with piles of old books or trailing houseplants or colorful handknit throws. Emmy Wilson's house basically just has a lot of *junk*.

She whisks away what looks like a pile of dirty laundry so I can sit down at a kitchen table that is covered with breakfast dishes even though it's after eleven. While I sit down, murmuring my thanks, my three oldest children skulk in the doorway and Rose superglues herself to my side. I've warmed to Emmy, but I don't think my children have warmed to this home. Not yet, anyway.

"Coffee?" Emmy asks and then starts filling the kettle without waiting for a reply. She glances at my children, who have been pretty much silent, and then barks, "Ben! Alice! Get in here."

Out of the corner of my eye, I see Bethany cringe and I know what she's thinking. There's nothing more *awkward* than parents who force their children to get along and assume it will all be easy and fine if they just push them together.

"Coming," a male voice calls, and then a boy—a man, really—comes into the kitchen. He's wearing an untucked plaid flannel shirt and faded jeans, and he has the same messy, straw-colored hair as his mother, along with vivid green eyes. Topping six feet with a farmer's muscular build, he's got a rugged appeal that I'm pretty sure no boy in Bethany's class back in Princeton had in the slightest. Her eyes widen and her cheeks go pink.

"Where's Alice?" Emmy demands as she plops the kettle on the stove and wipes her hand on an old dishrag.

"She's changing Eleanor."

Emmy sighs. "Well, have her bring the baby to me and then show these kids around," she orders, and my three oldest all wilt a little, because they've now become a burden, i.e., social suicide. I try to give William an encouraging smile, but he's staring straight ahead like he's enduring the seventh circle of hell.

"Sure," Ben says easily, glancing at my three with frank curiosity. "I was just going to check on the foal that was born last night. You guys want to come?"

"A foal?" Rose cries, unsticking herself from my side. "You mean a baby horse?"

Ben smiles, slow and easy. "Yup. That's exactly what I mean."

"Um..." Bethany has to clear her throat. "Yeah, sure, thanks."

I watch the three of them troop off, followed by Peter and Polly, fourteen-year-old fraternal twins, Carolyn, who is ten, and finally sixteen-year-old Alice, who has the same straw-colored hair but long and frizzy, and an abundance of freckles. Emmy tells me their names and ages as they walk by, and Alice hands her a disgruntled-looking baby before following the others outside.

"They'll be fine," Emmy tells me as she puts baby Eleanor in an old wooden chair and hands her a spoon which she begins banging with a lot of enthusiasm—and noise. "I saw that look of terror on your son's face," she adds with a chuckle, "and I don't blame him. Meeting new people is always so hard, especially at that age, but my seven are friendlier than most, maybe because they never went to school." She reaches for a bag of coffee beans and starts loading them into a hand grinder.

"You homeschool them all?" I ask. No wonder the kitchen is a mess.

"Yes and no," Emmy replies as she starts grinding. "Ben graduated last year and he's now doing a business course online. Alice is in online school, as is Peter. Polly pretty much does her own thing, now that we've come to an understanding." She gives me a look full of humor. "She doesn't like anyone to teach her anything, which makes getting an education somewhat difficult." She shrugs as she pours the ground beans into a French press. "But we figure it out. Carolyn is only ten, so I'm stuck with her, and then little Sammy, when the time comes, and of course Eleanor eventually, although who knows what I'll be up for then. Ah, here he is!"

I turn to see the grimy-faced toddler from the window standing in the kitchen doorway. He's wearing a pajama shirt, red rainboots, and no pants.

"Everyone's outside looking at the foal, Sammy," Emmy tells her son. "Do you want to go find them?"

He nods, sticking his thumb in his mouth and she gives him an encouraging smile as he makes his way across the kitchen and then disappears outside.

"And now a little peace and quiet," she announces, and whisks the spoon away from Eleanor, who lets out an indignant squeal before Emmy dumps her a handful of Cheerios onto the tray of her high chair.

"I'm in awe," I tell her with a little laugh. "How do you manage so much? I feel overwhelmed, and I only have four kids."

"Well, look at the state of my kitchen," Emmy replies. "Or my laundry room. Or anything around here. It's total chaos." She says this happily enough. "But we survive."

"Are you from around here?" I ask, and she nods.

"Born and bred. I left for WVU when I was eighteen and then a fancy secretarial job in Richmond for two years. Got my heart broken by a city boy and came hightailing back to my high school sweetheart, Ed. He'd gone to WVU, too, but we'd broken up by then. I wanted *space*." She laughs ruefully. "Then he got a job back here, working for the Division of Forestry, which is just a fancy way of saying he's a logger." She lets out another laugh, this one loud and merry. "He hates it when I say that. No, he does a lot of other stuff. Woodland management, stewarding resources, that kind of thing. Anyway, we reconnected when I came home to decide whether I was a city or country girl at heart, and I ended up staying without ever figuring out the answer to that question. Milk? It's from our own." She proffers a mug of coffee, a glass bottle of milk poised over it.

"Sure, thanks."

She pours in a generous splash and then hands me my mug, which I take with murmured thanks. I am intrigued by this woman, her chaotic life, her cheerful disposition, the fact that by her own admission she still doesn't seem to quite know where she belongs, and yet she's clearly thriving here, among all the kids and the mess.

It makes me think that maybe I can, too, especially if I can make a few friends.

"So," Emmy asks, levelling me with a look that is both humorous and blunt, "how hard is it?"

For a second, I think of prevaricating, even though I know exactly what she means. Then I decide her own cheerful honesty deserves a similar response. "It shouldn't be hard at all," I tell her. "We *chose* this, and we've been incredibly fortunate with being able to afford to do it at all." She frowns, and I hope I didn't misunderstand her. She was talking about homesteading, I hope?

"Just because you chose something doesn't mean it isn't hard," she remarks as she takes a sip of her coffee.

"That's true," I acknowledge. "It just feels like I can't complain when I knew what I was getting into."

She laughs then, a loud, rich sound. "Honey, I don't think there's a woman alive who knows what she's getting into. When I married Ed?" She glances around the messy kitchen, with its dirty dishes and piles of laundry, the wallpaper peeling off one corner and the kitchen faucet dripping in a way that suggests it will never be fixed. "If I'd known I was going to have seven kids and live in a house with a leaky roof and sagging floors and a cat that was *meant* to be outside only, but we gave up that fight long ago..." She trails off in a sigh as said cat jumps onto the tray of Eleanor's high chair. The baby squeals as the cat swishes its tail in her face. "Well, I would have married him anyway, of course," Emmy resumes. "But I might have thought about it awhile first."

"This started out as Josh's dream," I answer hesitantly, "but it's both of ours now."

She nods sagely, her eyes sparkling with humor. "Of course it is."

I smile shamefacedly at that. "Is it so obvious that I'm the weak link?"

Emmy leans over and grabs my hand. "Don't call yourself that. You, like many other good women before you, are the voice of reason and sense. Many a man would have headed west in his wagon and died out there somewhere in the Rockies if there hadn't been a woman to bake the bread and manage the kids and remind him that you can't cross the Platte River with skittish oxen."

I'm not totally familiar with the reference, but I think I get the gist of what she's talking about. Josh needs me to bring him back down to earth. I've known that all along, but I haven't always *felt* it, especially when I feel like I'm keeping him back with my worries and doubts.

"But," Emmy continues with a certain gleam in her eye, "many a woman needed a man to help her dream bigger than the next meal or a fractious baby."

As if on cue, Eleanor lets out a warning squawk, like she's thinking about crying but hasn't decided yet. I smile at Emmy in agreement.

Yes, Josh and I balance each other out. I've felt that for a long time, but I'm only just realizing that we balanced each other out in *my* world of safe suburbia. Do we still manage that when we're in what is still essentially Josh's world? When I'm the one who struggles not to still feel anxious and disappointed, restless for what we don't have, or even what we do?

Yes, we chose this life. We both did. I know I needed the reminder.

"Life isn't linear," Emmy says as she reaches over to haul Eleanor out of her high chair. "Or circular. Or diagonal, for that matter, or anything where it's a continuous upward trajectory."

My eyes practically cross as I try to imagine all the shapes of what life isn't. "So what *is* life, then?" I ask with a laugh.

"Hmm, I don't know," Emmy replies thoughtfully. "A squiggly line, maybe? All I'm saying, there are highs and lows and plenty of flat lining too, when you feel like nothing ever changes." She sighs, and for a second her air of cheerful humor drops, and I want to ask her what struggles she might be facing, but I'm not quite brave enough.

"Anyway," she says, settling Eleanor on her hip. "Shall we go see the foal? Nothing like a baby animal to cheer you up."

Outside is just as messy as inside, with various tools and toys scattered about—a wheelbarrow, a tricycle, a homemade archery target, an axe stuck into a stump. Chickens peck the ground and flap their wings, and clothes pegged to a line flutter in the breeze, looking like tattered flags.

"Mom, come look," Rose calls excitedly from the door of the big red barn. "It's a baby horse and it was just born *yesterday*."

"Carolyn's our horsewoman," Emmy says as she strolls into the barn. "Although Alice rides, too. How are they doing, honey?"

I blink in the dim lighting of the barn that smells of hay and animal, not an unpleasant aroma. The kids are all gathered around a stable where a wobbly-legged foal, about as high as Rose, is sniffing the ground with a velvety nose.

"Oh..." My voice softens and my heart melts. There really is nothing cuter than a baby animal, whatever it is. I think I'd coo even at a baby crocodile.

"Isn't she cute?" Rose exclaims, grabbing my hand. "Can we get a horse? Baby horses are cuter than baby chickens."

Especially since, three weeks on, our chicks are less perfect puffballs and more gangly, skinny chickens, all claw and beak.

"I don't know, Rose," I answer honestly. "None of us ride." I'm still not entirely convinced about getting a cow, although the milk in my coffee did taste fresh and creamy.

I glance around at all the children—Emmy's seven and my four, all of them enthralled by the little foal. The ages match up even if the genders don't—William is studiously avoiding both sixteen-year-old Alice and fourteen-year-old Polly, and Bethany is as far from Ben as she can get, although I notice she keeps slipping him covert glances. Jack is talking with Peter, Polly's twin, and ignoring Carolyn, who is closer to his age. Despite all that, there is a feeling of camaraderie among them that I am grateful for.

By the time we head home an hour later, after Emmy has produced homemade oatmeal cookies from a battered tin as well as a jug of freshly squeezed lemonade and all the children devour both, I am feeling as if all is right with the world.

The sun is shining, the air is warm, and next week we are intending to plant our garden. Sow the seeds of our life here, which is what feels like happened today.

"Can we come again?" Rose asks as she skips to the car.

"I think so," I reply, glancing at my older three. "What do you guys think?"

"Yeah, they were nice," Bethany says, which sounds lukewarm, but I know, considering the situation, is high praise.

"William?" I ask. "Jack?"

Both my boys shrug and nod, also high praise considering the circumstances. "Yeah, okay," they half-mumble.

As I drive toward home, I find I can't stop smiling.

Chapter Seventeen

After the successful visit to the Wilsons, I decide I really need to make more of an effort to visit my other neighbors—Lily and Robbie Pepper, the mysterious Miss Barbara, and even Hooch, who, although he's dropped by our house several times a week, I haven't yet been to visit him.

So a few days after the very successful visit to the Wilsons, I make three loaves of banana bread and then, accompanied by a curious Rose, start on my rounds. First is Miss Barbara at the top of the valley—or holler, a word I can't even think without feeling self-conscious—just half a mile up the road, and down a deeply rutted drive to a small white clapboard house surrounded by a wild garden and two large greenhouses. I told Bethany I was going to pay Miss Barbara a visit, and her response was deeply suspicious.

"Why?" she demanded as she looked up from *The Complete Herbalist*. "Are you checking up on me?"

"Is there anything to check up on?" I asked lightly, and she scowled.

"Of course not. But I don't like you spying on my friends."

I nearly choked on that; Barbara was sixty-seven years old. "She's our neighbor," I reminded my daughter lightly. "I want to meet her, regardless of your relationship."

Bethany harrumphed and went back to her book, and so here I am with a loaf of banana bread and a good deal of curiosity. I'm not sure what I'm expecting—a woman wearing a lot of scarves and bangles and smelling of patchouli, maybe—but Miss Barbara is not it.

She answers the dress dressed in yoga pants and a zip-up fleece, the kind of activewear ensemble I might have seen back in Princeton. Her neat silver bob and discreet gold hoops also are more reminiscent of my old life than anything I've encountered here. Another stereotype toppled, I realize with an inwardly shamefaced grimace. Why, in Wildflower Valley, should I expect people to be one way or the other? Admittedly, considering how much time my daughter has been spending with Miss Barbara, I'm relieved she's not the hash-brownie hippy of Josh's and my nebulous fears.

"You must be Bethany's mom," she greets me warmly, holding open the screen door to let me come in. "And let me guess," she says, turning to Rose. "You must be Rose, and this, I think…" She pauses dramatically before proclaiming, "this must be Bruce."

Yes, Rose is still carrying Bruce around everywhere she goes. I'd be worried except I think she's doing it out of stubbornness rather than any concerning attachment. Last week, Jack teased that she must not like him anymore because she wasn't carrying him around, and she immediately ran and got him and sat him next to her at the dinner table. Josh and I agreed to just wait it out.

Now she beams at Miss Barbara, delighted. "Yes," she announces proudly. "This is Bruce."

"Isn't he handsome," Miss Barbara enthuses before shooting me a wryly amused look. I decide right then that we're going to be friends.

Over cups of green tea and banana nut cookies that are a little too healthy for my preference but tasty all the same, Miss Barbara fills us in on her life. She moved to Wildflower Valley when she was twenty-seven, after her parents died and left her with a small legacy, enough to buy this house and set up a yoga studio.

"It didn't take," she states with a frank smile. "Which isn't all that surprising, in this area, and especially forty years ago, when yoga was still seen as something a little out there." She shrugs as she reaches for another cookie. "But it didn't matter in the end, because I ended up falling in love with this place and having a garden instead. I'll give you the tour, if you like. You can see what Bethany's been up to, too."

"That sounds great," I reply. "Thank you," I add belatedly, "for taking Bethany under your wing. She came here with this big idea about doing something with herbs and it's just been… providential… that you live nearby and have been willing to teach her."

"Well, it's nice to have some company," Barbara says. "I haven't been lonely, exactly, but sometimes I've felt alone." She gives a smile that seems both defiant and a little shamefaced. "You get to my age, and you don't mind having someone around on occasion, but…" She smiles as she holds up one warning finger. "Only on occasion."

By the time Barbara has shown us around her extensive greenhouses and garden, naming all the herbs and their various uses that I try to remember but generally don't, it's afternoon and Rose is flagging a little. I listen as Barbara tells me how Bethany is helping her grind and distil some herbal remedies for her mail catalogue business—"it keeps my head above water, financially speaking, if only just". Eventually, we say our goodbyes and I drop Rose back at home before heading to my other visits.

I go to the Peppers first, on the other side of the valley, crossing the little wooden bridge over Sixpole Creek, still rushing strong with spring melt, and head back up the steep hillside that is now covered in bluebells and spreading asters, at least that's what I think they are, according to our wildflower book. They've turned the wooded hills into a sea of violet, and the beech and maple trees are in full, bright green leaf.

I pull into the Peppers' drive, bumping carefully over the rocks and ruts, wincing as something scrapes the bottom of my car. Maybe I should have taken the truck. As I come around the corner, my breath comes out in a rush because the Peppers' homestead is a far cry from any of the ones I've seen so far in our time in Wildflower Valley, and more like the kind Hooch warned me about, the kind of place people abandon, filled with trash and the inevitable, accompanying rats.

I park the van and sit there for a moment, surveying the tiny shack with its sagging front porch, a broken window that's been boarded up with plywood, and a roof covered with tar paper. It's the saddest looking place I've seen, and I'm glad I didn't bring Rose.

Slowly I get out of the car, clutching my banana bread to my chest. I'm really not sure who—or what—I'll find inside, but the Peppers are our neighbors, and I'm determined to be friendly.

The steps creak in protest as I mount them and then knock a little timidly on the front door. No one answers, and part of me is tempted to leave the banana bread and tiptoe away.

I resist that cowardly impulse, though, and knock again. While I'm waiting for someone to answer, I glance around the yard; there are a couple of old pickup trucks that look like their engines are in various states of disarray, and I recall what Hooch said about Robbie Pepper being good with motors. He's not, I can already see, so great with house repairs. I am just considering whether to leave after all when I hear footsteps and then the front door opens just a crack.

"Hello?" The woman's voice is suspicious, a little sullen, and I am taken aback. Everyone I've met here, I realize, has been so friendly, that blatant unfriendliness feels like a shock.

"Hi, I'm your new neighbor, Abby Bryant," I say cheerfully. "Are you... Lily?" I can't even see her face; she only opened the door enough to reveal a glimpse of her cheek and some dirty blond hair.

"Yeah, I'm Lily," she says in the same guarded tone. She doesn't offer anything more, and she doesn't open the door any wider.

For a second, I am at a loss, but then I persevere. "Oh, well, I brought you some banana bread," I inform her uncertainly. "I'm sorry it's taken me so long to come by, but my husband Josh and I have wanted to introduce ourselves to all our neighbors in Wildflower... Holler..." I manage to say the word.

For a second there's only silence. "Oh, well..." Lily finally says, and then trails off into more silence.

This has to rank as one of the most awkward conversations I've ever had, but underneath the frustration at this young woman's unfriendliness is a growing concern. Hooch said Lily was only about twenty or so. Living in this rundown place alone with her husband and, it seems, not much support...

Am I being paranoid, to be worried for her health, maybe even her safety?

"Shall I just leave it here?" I finally ask, a little desperately. "Or if you want to take it..."

I trail off, waiting for Lily's reply.

"You can just leave it there," she says, and she watches me from the crack in the door, no more than a glint of green eye, as I put the loaf on the porch and then, with no real alternative, head back down the porch steps.

"It was nice meeting you," I call to her, and my only reply is the door closing with a firm sounding click.

Oh-kay. I'm still reeling from the bizarre encounter as I head back across Sixpole Creek to Hooch's place, where I am seriously hoping for a friendlier welcome.

I've never been past the front gate of Hooch's homestead, but I do notice that the half-rotting wood is hanging from rusted hinges as I drive by. Hooch has been so helpful to us over the last month, stopping by to lend a hand to just about anything—digging up a rock, putting in a fence post, stacking wood. He also almost always brings a little gift, too—a pot of honey from his mother's bees, a sack of corn for the chicken's feed, and once an unlabeled mason jar of moonshine that I put far back in the pantry.

Because of all this, I suppose I am expecting a small, neat holding like the Hoffenbergers, but with less money or show. As I round the curve of his drive, though, I find instead a house that's better than the Peppers' place, but only just. Hooch's family home is small, weathered, and while it's clearly tended, it's also obvious there's not a lot of money for such maintenance. One window is covered with sheet plastic, and the roof is well-patched rather than completely reroofed, as it so obviously needs. Hooch's gifts to us seem all the more precious and poignant as I now regard the state of his own affairs. I realize I don't even know if he has a job; he can't be much more than mid-thirties.

Slowly, holding my loaf of banana bread, I get out of the car.

I knock once on the door before calling, "Hooch? It's Abby. I thought I'd stop by."

There's no response, and again I am tempted to leave the loaf and tiptoe away. But I don't, because this is Hooch, someone who has already been a good friend to us, and I want to be a good friend back.

"Hooch?" I call again.

After what feels like forever but is probably only a minute or two, I hear footsteps, the creak of floorboards. Then Hooch opens the door to regard me blearily. The smell of moonshine rolls off him, nearly making me choke.

"Oh, Miss Abby..." he says, sounding regretful. "I didn't know you were comin'."

"I thought I'd stop by," I manage, holding out the banana bread. "I brought this."

Hooch runs a skinny wrist under his nose. "Ah, you shouldn't have," he says, still sounding regretful. He looks around him dolefully. "I'm not much in the mind of visitors..."

"I don't mind, Hooch," I say gently. I feel an ache of sorrow for him that I don't entirely understand—his indefatigable optimism and the fact that he's been hitting the moonshine pretty hard at two in the afternoon are hard to reconcile, and yet here they are, right in front of me.

"Well..." His shoulders slump. He suddenly looks, despite his grizzled appearance, very young. "If you're sure..."

"I'm sure," I tell him, and I am. Hooch disappears back into the house, and I follow him, picking my way across the trash-strewn floor, trying not to wrinkle my nose at the smell of beer, sweat, and rotten food.

Inside, the cramped living room is taken over by a sagging sofa and a large screen TV and not much else. Hooch stands in the middle of the room, looking dejected.

"Can I offer you something, Miss Abby?" he asks, and my heart aches for him,

I'm about to say I don't need anything when it occurs to me that having Hooch actually do something for someone might be the best thing for now.

"A cup of tea would be lovely," I tell him, and he looks surprised, and then shyly pleased.

Ten minutes later, we're seated in a tiny kitchen that is in just as bad state as the living room, a cup of dubious-looking tea in front of me, along with a slumped Hooch.

"How are you, Hooch?" I ask quietly, and he slumps further.

"Oh, you know, Miss Abby, sometimes I get in a way," he admits, his head hanging low. "A terrible way. I get so lonesome, you see. My momma, she's in Buckholt with my sister Daisy, and my other brothers and sisters, they've gone even further away... 'cept my brother Kenneth, he's in Denmar... that's a prison, that is, a certified correctional center, and I don't see him much at all." He sighs, shaking his head sorrowfully.. "Poor Kenneth," he laments, before hanging his head. "But maybe I'm not much better, with you seeing me as I am..." he says mournfully, his chin nearly touching his chest.

As sorry as I feel for Hooch in this moment, alone in his family home with the mess of his life all around him, I am sensing that self-pity is a well-worn groove he falls into, as we all often do, and he could benefit from a talking-to as much as he could a hug.

"I suppose it's hard, not having family close by," I tell him bracingly, "but you've got plenty of neighbors, Hooch, and you're a very good neighbor yourself. Why, I don't know what we'd have done without you, on moving day, or pretty much any day since." Without realizing I was doing it, I've fallen into the West Virginian drawl. Maybe it was inevitable. "You saved us, and that's a fact," I tell him.

Hooch lifts his head, his whole expression brightening. "Oh, Miss Abby..."

"Now, come on," I say, reaching over to give his hand a firm pat. "Enough of the moonshine, as good as I know it must be. Why don't we get this kitchen cleaned up, and maybe you can have a cup of tea or coffee yourself, and then if you like you can join us for dinner. We need your advice as we're planting next week! How does all that sound?"

For a second, he looks near tears. "You mean it?" he asks, sounding both incredulous and hopeful.

"Of course I mean it," I reply in the same bracing tone. "Why wouldn't I?" I don't let him answer that question as I start cleaning up the kitchen, and Hooch, giving me a sad, apologetic sort of smile, joins me. As we start washing dishes, chatting companionably about spring planting and how our chicks are getting on, I realize that I needed this almost as much as Hooch obviously did.

Since moving here, I've met quite a few very lovely people who have been both helpful and inspirational, but until this moment I never felt like anyone in Wildflower Valley, outside of my own family, *needed* me. I'm glad it seems as if Hooch does, even if I hope a strong cup of coffee and a clean kitchen might be enough to help him on his way.

Chapter Eighteen

Three days before the end of April, we plant. It feels like a momentous occasion. I've been hoarding seed packets, far more than we could use, and we have a ton—literally—of compost left in a pile by the barn, should we need it. The chicken run is completed, and our eight gangly chicks are now pecking the dirt inside it, seeming happy enough with their new lodgings. The kitchen addition is taking shape, and next week Tony said they could start on the bedrooms.

Life is moving on, hopefully, relentlessly, and it's time to put seeds into earth and pray that they grow. It feels right, this season of new birth; on Easter Sunday, we all showed up at Grace Church for the second time and were welcomed like old friends. Rose and Jack participated in the Easter egg hunt after the service, and I'm both ashamed and proud to admit that Jack found far too many eggs and refused to give any up without some serious duress.

Out of the corner of my eye, I saw Bethany and Ben talking; Bethany looked diffident, Ben at ease. William was avoiding the opposite sex like the plague, but he did wave at Peter, and it seems that Jack and Carolyn have, since they first stuck their tongues out at each other a month ago, become mortal enemies, which probably means they'll get married one day.

BOTH FEET IN

In any case, it was nice to feel a part of something, even if I still didn't know most people's names and I was battling with impostor syndrome, since I wouldn't exactly call us church-going people, although maybe that's what we're becoming.

All in all, there's no reason to hesitate. I'm not sure why I've built up planting in my mind; maybe because it's the literal version of putting down roots. Maybe also because I'm afraid if nothing comes up from the tiny seeds we're scattering in the earth, I'll feel like our whole life here is a failure. Not that I'm being melodramatic or anything, but a lot is riding on this vegetable garden, and not just because, according to Josh and William's calculations, it will feed Rose and half of Jack for the year.

The day we pick is sunny and warm, even by eight o'clock in the morning. I made us a fortifying breakfast of bacon and eggs and now we're all out in our fenced patch, gazing at the deep brown earth with a kind of reverence.

William has got our *Complete Vegetable Handbook* out like it's some sort of scripture, open in his hands as he intones,

"We plant the corn first, and then two weeks later the beans, and a week after that the squash."

We're hoping to try the three sisters method of planting the three together, so the beans twine around the corn stalks and provide nitrogen for the soil, while the squash gives ground coverage. Or so we've read. Now William tells us to plant the seeds one to two inches deep, and eight to twelve inches apart, in rows three feet apart. As Rose and I put the first seeds into soil, with her gently patting the earth over the tiny seed, it occurs to me that with this kind of spacing, Josh was probably right. Half an acre isn't that much.

It takes all morning just to plant the corn, moving slowly, letting

Rose pat the earth over each seed. Jack and Bethany, meanwhile, have started on the other end and are planting rows of spinach and lettuce, with William putting stakes to mark each row and Josh working one row ahead of them, creating furrows.

"Why are we planting spinach?" Jack asks as they finish their third row. "I don't even like it. I never eat it."

"It's good for you," I tell him, deciding to keep the fact that I've been sneaking it into spaghetti sauces since he was a baby from him, lest he think his whole life was a lie.

Row by row, we work through the whole garden—spinach and lettuce, corn and carrots and cabbage, as well as our chitted potatoes. The tomatoes and cucumbers we started inside I bring outside to harden up before we transplant them.

At one point, as the sun shines down and we all keep working, Josh and I both straighten at the same time and meet each other's gazes. The kind of silent conversation that is only possible after twenty years of marriage goes between us.

Can you believe we actually did this?
Look at them out there, all working together.
We made the right choice.
Yes, we did.

Then we smile at each other and go back to our work.

Two days after our planting, Emmy's husband Ed shows up in his truck, with a trailer behind that holds something I didn't even know existed—a stump grinder. He's here on Emmy's request to help us finally take down the blighted trees in the orchard. He's even brought a brand new plum tree to get us started.

While we're all exclaiming over his kindness, Hooch rattles up in his truck, jumping out with enthusiasm and assuring us that he's always wanted to "try his hand" at a stump grinder. I have a special affection for Hooch after visiting him last week; after washing the dishes, we drove back to our house, and he played catch with Jack in the backyard while I started on dinner.

Soon enough, we're all out in the orchard, with Josh firing up the chainsaw with enthusiasm. It still seems a terrible tragedy to have to cut down every single tree, but I tell myself it means a fresh start for everyone—orchard included. It's good to have Ed Wilson, a proper forester, in charge of the whole operation, as we'd have no idea where to begin with any of it.

Halfway through, the Hoffenbergers arrive, ostensibly bearing gifts—in this case a bag of fresh spinach that Jack regards with dread—but mostly, I think, to check out what we're doing. I don't mind; neighborliness and nosiness go hand in hand here in the holler, it seems, and when Bill starts rolling up his sleeves to help shift the cut-up wood, I'm grateful.

While they're continuing in the orchard, I head back to the house to see what I can rustle up for lunch. I can't quite keep a note of pride from entering my voice as I casually take out a fresh loaf of bread to go with the baked beans that have been in the crock pot since dawn, assuring Allie we've got plenty to go around. A jar of peaches preserved in honey, courtesy of Miss Barbara, served with fresh cream from Emmy Wilson's milk cow round out a meal for all of us. I'm not quite Hoffenberger or Walker level of homesteading, but I feel like I'm getting there.

As they head back out to the orchard, Allie helps me wash up. Standing together at the sink, watching Hooch and Ed Wilson head back out with the others, I work up the nerve to say casually,

"I stopped by Lily and Robbie Peppers' the other day."

"Oh?" Allie's tone is, I fear, slightly forbidding.

"Yes… Lily answered the door, but she didn't let me in. She didn't actually open it." I glance at Allie. "She seemed… suspicious."

"Well, the Peppers like to keep to themselves."

"But she's so young," I protest. I haven't been able to stop thinking about Lily Pepper, only twenty years old, stuck in that rundown shack. "I'm worried about her."

"Worried?" Allie eyes me askance. "What's there to be worried about?"

"I just hope she's happy."

"I'm sure she's all right." Judging from Allie's tone, there is clearly a big difference between neighborliness and nosiness. "You'll find," she continues as she dries a plate, "that people around here help each other out the way we're doing today. But they also know when to keep to themselves if they need to. The Peppers don't want any help, or people poking around. Maybe they'll change their minds, but until they do, it's best to leave them to it."

"Fair enough," I murmur. I'm not itching to go back to the Peppers, and yet the sight of Lily's face through the crack of the door still worries me. She's only a couple of years older than Bethany. Maybe she needs some help, even if she is afraid to ask for it. But am I, stranger that I am, really the one to give it to her?

Chapter Nineteen

Over the next few weeks, life falls into a pleasing rhythm. Up at dawn to feed the chickens—they're eight weeks old now and we suspect, although aren't certain, that we have two roosters and six chickens—and work outside in a variety of projects. Josh and William are building a woodshed, and Jack is making a target for the bow and arrow he got at the feedstore in Buckholt, the next best thing, according to him, to a gun. I have transplanted my tomatoes and cucumbers and watch over them as tenderly as a mother hen with her chicks, cupping their green shoots with both hands, willing them to grow, while also anxiously awaiting the first seedlings to sprout of all the other things we've planted.

After a hearty breakfast, I sit down with Rose and Jack to get a little schooling done, although often we end up outside. The weather is gorgeous—warm without being too hot, a fresh breeze blowing, the whole world to discover. Homeschooling takes on a whole new definition—reading is out on a blanket on the lawn, science is pond dipping and observing the many tadpoles shooting around the murky water, stirring the mulchy leaves at the bottom to observe what emerges.

Bethany spends a good part of each day at Miss Barbara's, although she's also cultivated her own corner of the vegetable patch for various herbs, and we've squeezed a stillroom, ie, a closet, into our addition plans off the bedrooms, although I'm still not entirely sure what she'll use it for.

"Do you dry herbs," I asked her once, "or preserve them in oil?"

"It depends," she replied, and did not elaborate, I have a feeling because she wasn't entirely sure.

Amazingly, the kitchen construction is almost finished, a big, blank room with a huge picture window overlooking the back, ready for counters and cabinets to be installed. In the second week of May we take a family trip to the booming metropolis of Charleston, West Virginia to pick out a stove and fridge as well as decide on such crucial elements as light fixtures and splashbacks.

I'm both curious and apprehensive as to how we all will do in the city after six weeks in Wildflower Valley. Will we be shrinking back at all the traffic and noise, or will we all get to the hotel room and gleefully grab our devices like robots plugging into the matrix? That's what I'm really afraid of—that we'll slot back in all too easily, and forget all we've learned and more importantly, who we've become.

When I've gone into Buckholt for work, I've always checked my phone for messages or texts, and a few have trickled in from friends, asking how we are. I respond with a wry cheerfulness that I hope conveys our experience without being either smug or pathetic. Messages from friends aside, each time I go some part of me can't keep from scrolling, gorging on social media and celebrity news like an addict in need of a fix. I've done it less and less, thankfully, over the weeks, but the instinct is still there, and I want to root it out. I fear unlimited Wi-Fi in the Holiday Inn in Charleston isn't going to help me, never mind my children.

To my surprise, however, the internet isn't the main attraction of the hotel when we arrive; the pool is. I'm not sure Bethany has even checked her phone once since we arrived, and William forgot to bring his. It's both encouraging and faintly alarming, although I can't articulate why.

"This is what we wanted," Josh reminds me. "Kids unplugged. Enjoying nature."

"Or a swimming pool in a concrete courtyard," I quip. We're sitting by the poolside during the hotel's happy hour, sipping lurid-colored margaritas from plastic cups. It all feels pleasant but also strange. As I glance around at the other guests, I feel a little bit like an alien from another planet, or at least how I imagine one might feel, observing these bizarre customs, wondering if I'll pass as a local.

Which, I reflect, was a little bit how I felt when we first moved to West Virginia. Have I changed that much? Josh and I are still amateurs and beginners when it comes to homesteading, but I know that already I'm not who I was back in Princeton, which is a good thing... right?

At bedtime, with the six of us crammed into one suite, disaster strikes. I am just making up the sofa bed for Jack when Rose shrieks like she's been stabbed in the eye.

"I forgot *Bruce!*" she wails, and I can tell from the way her eyes are filling and her face is going red, I sense a massive meltdown is imminent.

"Bruce is holding down the fort at home," William says quickly, putting an arm around his little sister's shoulders in a way I don't think he ever would have, back in New Jersey. "He likes it there, you know. He's company for the chickens."

Rose eyes him distrustfully even as she leans into his shoulder.

"You guys could use a little time apart," Bethany chimes in.

"Bruce needs his space."

"What is that supposed to mean?" she cries, her voice wobbling, and my oldest daughter rolls her eyes.

"You're too old for a teddy bear," Jack tells Rose, more matter of fact than unkind. "And the way you carry him around everywhere is weird."

"It's not weird!" Rose shrieks, and her three siblings remain silent. Okay, so we're not at The Waltons-level of family unity and support, and I haven't been the only one who has found Rose's attachment to Bruce a little tiresome, but we are getting there. Kind of.

Eventually, Rose quiets down and the children all settle into bed, with Bethany reading by the light of her phone, which seems to be the only use she's had for it. Curious, I perch on the edge of her bed.

"You haven't wanted to check messages?" I ask, afraid that I might be treading in dangerous waters by even broaching the subject. "Or scroll on social media?"

"Nah." Bethany flips a page in her book. "I checked my messages earlier, and there wasn't much. I mean, people knew I was going off the grid, and basically, once you leave high school you're forgotten."

"You had some good friends, Bethany," I protest, and she gives me a direct look.

"Yes, but they were situational," she says, clearly unfazed by this admission. "Like, we were friends because we were in marching band, or both wanted to get into good colleges, or whatever. As soon as that changes…" She shrugs. "The friendship pretty much dies. It's okay," she assures me, reaching over to pat my hand. "I'm over it."

I am silent, absorbing this. It saddens me how swiftly relationships can be forgotten, but at the same time I understand it. The messages from my own friends, six weeks on, have trickled to pretty much nothing. Vague promises to visit over the summer aren't, I'm pretty sure, going to materialize.

"What about friends here?" I ask, and Bethany arches an eyebrow.

"What friends?" she asks, only semi-joking, and I can't keep from wincing.

"The Wilsons..."

"They're nice," she allows, "but we don't know them really well yet."

"But you might—"

"Don't get any ideas," she warns me, wagging a finger. "I could see you pairing me up with Ben as soon as he walked through the door."

I think my daughter was the one doing that, but I remain silent on that point. "Alice seems nice," I say instead, and Bethany nods.

"Yeah, she's okay."

This is, I hope, high praise rather than something dismissive. Sensing my daughter's growing reticence to discuss her social life or lack thereof, I decide to leave it for now. I lean over and drop a quick kiss on her forehead, which she accepts with bemused surprise.

"Okay, well I just wanted to check in," I tell her. "Make sure you're happy."

She smiles, meeting my gaze. "I'm good."

"Good."

I rise from her bed and consider having the same kind of check-in with William, but he's already snuggled in bed, and I decide it can wait. Rose is asleep and Josh had a chat with Jack, so I think we're all covered, which, as a parent, is always a good feeling.

"All good?" Josh asks as I slip into bed next to him.

I smile and snuggle in. "All good."

The next day, we spend an inordinate amount of time debating such essential topics as what color tile for a backsplash and whether we want dimmer switches. We've already picked out a huge fridge as well as a six-burner stove, and the amounts for these items are eye-watering and make me nervous.

"Abby, relax," Josh tells me after he hands over our credit card. "This was all in the budget."

It *was*, but since we've gone over the budget in several other areas, it doesn't *feel* like it was. And the fact remains that the money we made off our house is steadily dwindling, and my twenty hours of work a week is not covering our household expenses. So yes, as we buy several four-figure appliances, I'm feeling nervous.

I'm also feeling like having the designer kitchen I once dreamed of isn't that important anymore. If I'm honest, I went into this whole homesteading adventure imagining I'd have a kitchen—and even a life—like the family we followed on YouTube, which is admittedly a rather shallow and juvenile way of planning my life, but I suppose everyone falls into that trap to some degree.

But now that I'm in a kitchen showroom planning that dream space, I realize it doesn't matter nearly as much as I thought it did. Yes, I want a kitchen that serves its purpose and more importantly is a welcoming space for both family and friends, but the sales assistant trying to convince us of the importance of a seamless sink or under cabinet lighting makes me feel like I was chasing the trappings of life rather than the truth.

Josh must sense this, because two hours into our shopping expedition—all four kids have surrendered to various devices, lounging around the showrooms—gazes glued to screens—he asks,

"Abby? Are you okay?"

"I'm fine." I pause before admitting apologetically to both my husband and the saleswoman, "I'm just not sure about all this."

"All what?" Josh asks cautiously. He knows me well enough to suspect I might be having yet another existential crisis about the trajectory of our life, but for once I'm not.

"I don't care so much about these details," I confess. "I'm glad we have a big kitchen, but it doesn't have to be state-of-the-art. I just want it to be a place where we can cook and eat and have people over." I've promised the Hoffenbergers and the Wilsons that we'll host them both when the kitchen is finished, and there's a long line of people from church who would definitely welcome an invitation.

"You... don't?" Josh sounds gobsmacked now as well as cautious.

"No." In fact, I am realizing that I'd rather have Emmy Wilson's messy, shabby kitchen than one that is all soulless gloss and chrome. "I just want a friendly, functional space."

A smile of relief breaks over my husband's face. "Okay," he says. "Well that makes things easier, I guess."

An hour later, we've chosen everything we need to, foregoing state-of-the-art for sensible, and we treat ourselves to lunch at Cracker Barrel and a stop at Costco to load up on supplies before heading back to Wildflower Valley. I think we're all glad to leave the city behind, which is a good feeling. Hooch took Max in and the Hoffenbergers are keeping an eye on the chickens, and while I'm certainly grateful for good neighbors, I just want to be back home. I miss Max and our chickens, the sun setting over the pond and the saplings in our orchard, the sound of the wind whispering through the trees.

I think everyone must feel the same, for there is a collective sigh of relief as Josh pulls up our steep drive, and there is our little house, looking a little bigger with the addition out front; next week the builders will start on the bedrooms.

"I'll go get Max from Hooch," Josh says, as Rose runs out to check on the chickens. I'm hauling in our luggage with William when I hear Bethany call in what I am unsure is excitement or alarm, "*Mom!*"

I head out to the back stoop, shielding my eyes from the fading sunlight as I squint at Bethany in the back of our vegetable patch. "Beth...?"

"My lavender came up!" she calls, and now I can tell it is definitely excitement in her voice. "And lots of other things too."

"I think the chickens are *fluffier*," Rose calls from the chicken run, where she is sitting in the dirt and letting the chickens cluck around her.

Laughing, I head out back. Bethany is right—in the two days we've been gone, our garden has grown, if only a little. Tender green shoots have appeared in admittedly rather wobbly lines, the first sign that our efforts have worked. It feels like a genuine miracle, to witness these tiny plants that will grow into potatoes, tomatoes, cucumbers, peppers, and more, now all barely buds.

"I'm going fishing!" Jack calls as he catapults down the hill toward the pond. One of the things we got at Costco were a couple of fishing rods.

"Jack, have you ever even fished before?" William calls from the back stoop in exasperation. Jack shrugs, unbothered, while William rolls his eyes before getting his own fishing rod. From the chicken run, Rose giggles in delight as she is tickled by one of our chickens, and then Josh comes around the corner of the house, followed by Max barking joyfully.

As I stand in my nascent vegetable garden, the sun setting over the green-tinted hills, my family all around me, I feel, right down into my bones, that all is right with the world.

Chapter Twenty

For two weeks, life is simple and sweet. The days remain sun-soaked, so our only real challenge is watering all our burgeoning plants and making sure they thrive, which they seem to. Josh and William finish building the woodshed, and Jack spends his days fishing or practicing archery or exploring in the woods. Rose has become mistress of the chickens, and since the weather is so good, I abandon homeschooling completely to spend more time in the garden.

Bethany divides her days between her own patch of garden and Miss Barbara's, and when the internet is finally installed, with surprisingly little fanfare, she starts working on completing her schoolwork so she can actually have a high school diploma. The other kids aren't too bothered about access to the internet, in part because it's simply too slow to do much more than look things up. Social media and YouTube videos lag terribly, which is probably a good thing—for all of us.

In any case, we're all too busy to do much more with the internet than google the odd yet necessary fact related to our new lives—when to thin carrots, how to fox-proof our chicken coop, and, for Jack, at what age you're allowed to shoot a gun.

"What do you want a gun for?" I ask him one day, exasperated, amused, and mildly alarmed by his obsession.

"To shoot things," Jack replies, like it's obvious, which I suppose it is.

"What do you want to shoot?" I ask with some trepidation.

"Things," he replies, and chooses not to elaborate.

"We should get a gu at some point," Josh tells me later. "We can keep it in a locked cabinet but living out in the country... most people have something. Usually several somethings."

I know that full well; part of our tour of the Hoffenbergers' place was a locked gun cabinet in their office. Hooch proudly "packs", as he says, and Bethany told me even Miss Barbara has a shotgun "to scare away critters". I'm pretty sure we're the only residents of Wildflower Valley who aren't carrying, but generally I'm okay with that, even though I know what Josh is suggesting makes sense.

"I'll think about it," I tell him, and he just smiles.

All in all, the days seem as if they pass in a golden haze of hard work and enjoyment; with the internet, I can now work from home, and I turn the attic space into a makeshift office, and Josh even installs an air conditioner, because now that it's nearing the end of May, the days are hot.

Evenings are spent on our brand-new back porch, watching the sun set over the pond. We go to church on Sundays, and Emmy Wilson invites us for lunch after, where she serves biscuits and gravy, fried ramps, or wild leeks, and peach cobbler for dessert.

The kids all get along, mostly, with only the occasional awkward silence or stutter, but overall it's fine, probably because there are simply so many of them, and I hope one day they'll all be firm friends... or who knows, maybe even something more. Bethany, I notice still blushes every time she sees Ben.

I talk to my dad about visiting again, maybe even for good, although our contractor Tony doesn't think they'll be done with the whole job until August at the earliest. They're making good progress with the extra bedrooms and bathroom, and in any case we've all become used to the constant sawing and hammering, or almost. August still can't come soon enough, but it's not driving me crazy the way I once feared it would. I don't know if that's because I've changed or something else has, but I'm glad that I have mostly held onto my equanimity.

And then it starts to rain.

At first, it's welcome, because the days have been so hot and dry, and a day of rain means the builders don't come, and we all get to stay inside, enjoying the quiet, the way the rain streaks down the windows, the beauty of the mist clinging to the trees that rise high above our little house. The second day, duty calls, and we all head out into the wet, to do the jobs that have to be done, even in the middle of a downpour. We're still good-natured about it, though, remarking at least several times a day how good all this rain is for the garden.

By day four, we're all getting a little stir crazy. Everything feels damp and even moldy. The rain is constant—alternating between a drizzle and a downpour, but keeping absolutely everything sopping wet. The floors become a sea of mud. The chickens look miserable and bedraggled, pecking the soggy ground. My little plants, still so young and fragile and tender, are looking miserable and bedraggled too, their young leaves weighed down by water. The builders haven't come for nearly a week, and it starts to feel like they might stay away forever.

After ten days of constant rain, the driveway becomes a river of mud. Everyone else in the valley, we've discovered, has dug ditches alongside their driveways for drainage, something the former owner did here, but hadn't maintained, and so the ditches on either side of the driveway are choked with dead leaves and weed and don't drain anything.

Josh manages to get to Buckholt in the truck for some essential supplies, but when he returns he can't even get up the road, and he parks the truck at the bottom and hikes up himself. We're stuck.

"What happens if we can't get out?" William asks, his voice laced with anxiety. "What if we starve?"

"We won't starve," I tell him calmly, although I am feeling pretty anxious myself. "We have plenty of food."

"We can always eat the chickens," Jack suggests cheerfully, while Rose screeches in protest and Bethany tells everybody to be quiet. Despite my lovely big kitchen that still doesn't have any appliances or counters, this house is feeling very small.

And still it rains. On the news, they talk about "the deluge" and how rivers are bursting their banks and low-lying towns are flooding. One day, when it's only drizzling, we all hike down to Hooch's house to check on him, since he's so close to Sixpole Creek, which is mud-brown and angry-looking, the water churning up dirt-flecked foam, rising to right under the bridge.

Hooch, however, is cheerful; his little house hasn't flooded, and even if it did, he assures us, he's got everything he needs on the second floor.

"And I can always pee out the window," he tells us, which is more information than I needed, but I'm glad for his sake he doesn't seem to be in danger.

"The rain will probably stop soon," I say, and Hooch gives me a kindly smile.

"Oh, I don't know about that, Miss Abby. We can get a real long wet spell in these parts, when the good Lord decides to send us a little rain."

I laugh weakly at that, and Hooch pats me on the arm.

"Y'all will be all right up at the top of the valley," he assures me.

We stop by the Hoffenbergers', as well, and while they are both delighted to see us and insist we come in for sweet tea and cookies, they assure us, a little smugly, that they haven't flooded in the five years since they've been here, and in any case, they've got everything they need, including sandbags and one hundred gallons of fresh water.

We leave feeling both reassured and worried that we might be in trouble ourselves.

"Should we get some fresh water?" William asks as the drizzle turns to yet another downpour. Right now, it feels like we have all the water we need.

As the days pass, my good humor, which I already have only a tenuous hold on, starts to slip away completely. I break out a thousand-piece puzzle we never did, and the kids all pick at it, doing a few pieces before losing interest, or snarling at someone for getting in their way while they're trying to work on it.

We lose our war against screens, and by day twelve I've given Rose and Jack unfettered access to the iPad, which unfortunately they have to share, which creates only more battles, which I knew it would, and ones I can barely bear to fight.

Life becomes tedious and then dispiriting. My low point is when the truck with all our kitchen fixtures and fittings finally arrives one morning, only to drive away again when they discover the muddy waterfall that is our driveway.

I stand at the front window, trying not to cry for the kitchen I insisted only weeks ago that I didn't even want as much as I'd thought I did. It seems like maybe I did want it, after all.

"They *will* come back," Josh comforts me with his arm around my shoulder. "This is just a little fall of rain." In a jokey voice, he sings a few lines from the *Les Misérables* song, but I'm uncharacteristically not in the mood.

It's *not* just a little fall of rain. It's a huge downpour, day after day.

My dispirited mood turns, inevitably, to the kind existential angst I'd really hoped I'd gotten over. If we all get so down by a couple days—okay, weeks—of rain, are we really the hardy homesteading type? Maybe we don't belong here.

I don't say as much to Josh, because I can tell he knows I'm thinking it because he goes into his chipper mode, jollying everyone along, cracking jokes at every opportunity, so much so that he puts us all even more on edge.

Sixteen days without a single dry day, I lie in bed staring out the window at the dank gray sky. It's dawn, but you wouldn't know it. I can't see a single ray of sunlight. I close my eyes and consider going back to sleep when Josh, who has already gotten up, comes in the bedroom, closing the door behind him with the kind of deliberate click that makes me open my eyes. He looks serious, too serious.

"What is it?"

"On the news they were talking about mudslides. Locally."

I rise onto my elbows, pushing my hair out of my face. "*Mudslides?*"

Hooch had mentioned, with relish, both mudslides and sinkholes and how they were likely in rainy weather like this. One old timer's cabin had disappeared right into the earth, which opened up like it did in Numbers and swallowed the Israelites up whole. I was both horrified and impressed by Hooch's Bible knowledge, because I certainly didn't know that story.

All in all, though, I hadn't paid him too much attention because Hooch liked to tell horror stories and insist, hand on heart, that they were absolutely true.

"How locally?" I ask Josh now. "And what exactly is a mudslide?" My image of a mudslide is a cocktail I used to drink in my twenties that tasted like a milkshake. "Is it just a lot of mud sliding down the hillside?" I ask. "Because that was already happening on our driveway."

"A *lot* of mud," Josh agrees heavily. "More than our driveway. Like, half the mountainside coming down and breaking off and covering everything." He runs a hand through his hair, looking more distressed than I've seen him in a long while. "Apparently, because the weather had been so dry before, the ground became hard and then a ton of rain in a short space of time can create the conditions for a mudslide. On the news they were talking about evacuating the region."

"Evacuating?" I stare at Josh in shocked horror. Despite everything he'd been saying, I didn't think he meant that level of danger. "You mean, a mudslide could fall right on our *house*?"

He shrugs. "We do live on a pretty steep slope."

"Yes, but..." I sit up to gaze unseeingly out the window. "Where would we go? And what about the chickens? If we leave... I mean, for how long? We can't just *abandon* everything we've worked for here."

I realize, despite my depression turning to existential angst about whether we belong here, I really *don't* want to leave. Not even for a potential mudslide.

"We also don't want to get buried alive in mud," Josh points out, without his usual humor. I think he's actually stone-cold serious. For him, this isn't some far-fetched what-if—it's a real possibility.

Suddenly panicked, I start to scramble out of bed. "So where do we go?" I ask as I throw on clothes. My mind is racing, and I am starting to feel genuinely, deeply afraid, like a mountain of mud might fall from the sky straight on top of us in the next five minutes. "Wait..." I stop, one arm in my sleeve, as I stare at him. "Josh, we can't go anywhere. We can't get down the drive."

"The truck is at the bottom," he reminds me. "We can take that. Drive to Buckholt, maybe, and stay in a hotel for a few days."

"And the chickens?"

He shrugs. "We take them with us, I guess?"

I am trying to picture us all crammed into the old pickup truck with eight chickens and Max in the back. And what hotel, even in West Virginia, would accept such guests?

I shake my head slowly. "Maybe we should just take our chances here."

"Abby..." Josh frowns unhappily. "*Look* out there."

I walk to the window and gaze out at the backyard, a view that has become so familiar and comforting over the last two months. The vegetable garden and lawn are verdant and awash with puddles, and the chicken run is a veritable swamp. I clock all that, and then I raise my gaze to the hillside above, dense with trees. Surely they'll keep any mud from sliding down too far, if it should in fact come to that?

Then, as Josh and I are watching, some dirt breaks off from the slope and showers the ground beneath it. It doesn't look *too* bad, but then it happens again, and again, in different places, showering the ground below with dirt and debris.

And as we still stare, silent and wary, a tree, a young sapling, starts to bend. I don't understand why until I see the mud, far more than the bits we saw showering down before, begins to cascade down the mountain, almost as if the earth is collapsing on itself. Then I realize it is.

I watch, completely aghast, as a tree at least twenty feet tall topples like a bent matchstick.

The mudslide is happening right now, right here in Wildflower Holler.

Chapter Twenty-One

"We've got to go!" Josh suddenly roars, springing into action while I can only stare, utterly horrified, as the mud continues to slide down the mountain, gathering trees and debris along the way, a brown, rock-strewn tidal wave. "To the basement." Josh grips my shoulder hard. "Abby, come *on*!"

"The *basement*." I turn away from the terrible view, too shocked to process what I've just seen. I do not, I realize, want to be buried alive in my basement. "Aren't we meant to go to higher ground?" I feel like I've read that somewhere, or maybe I've seen it on some survival show, and the instinct is kicking in now, hard.

Impatiently, Josh gestures to the mountain behind our house. "Abby, what higher ground *is* there to go to right now? Come on, we've got to get to safety! Can't you hear it?"

And then I do—a low, distant roar, like the rushing of water. It is, I realize, the mud sliding down the hillside.

"Come *on*!" Josh yells.

"Dad, what's going on?" William calls sleepily from his bedroom, and Bethany grumpily moans for everyone to be quiet because she's trying to sleep, and I almost laugh, except I'm too scared.

This is really happening. We might lose everything we've worked for. We might lose our *lives*.

Suddenly I spring into motion, snatching a sleepy Rose from her bed while she wails for Bruce, shepherding a pale-faced Jack along with one hand on his shoulder. Josh rouses Bethany and Wiliam and we all head downstairs. No one asks for an explanation; the mood is too urgent for that. We don't have time to get anything—no food or water, no blankets or first aid kits. We hurtle down the basement steps with Max hard on our heels and then huddle on the damp floor while above us that muted roar continues, and we stare silently at each other, wide-eyed with fear.

"What's happening?" Bethany finally asks in a shaky voice, and Josh explains about the mudslide.

"Wait... are we going to be buried *alive*?" she screeches, looking truly terrified, which is pretty much how I feel at that prospect. As ways to go, it's pretty darn low down on my list. Maybe we should have gone to the second floor rather than the basement, although our house is so small, that doesn't seem like the safest choice, either. If the mudslide is taking down twenty-foot trees, it could take down our little house, too.

"We are not going to be buried alive," Josh says calmly, although I can tell by the stillness of his expression that he isn't entirely sure. But he was right; with the amount of time we had, there wasn't anywhere else to go.

"We could starve down here," William says gloomily. "Or die of thirst."

"No, we won't," Josh says in the same reasonable voice. "We've got plenty of food down here that's stored in the pantry, and there's a sink for running water. And if the well doesn't work, we've got several cases of bottled water down here, too. I bought them the last time I went to Costco."

"You did?" I am admiring as well as grateful.

"And I packed an emergency box," Josh continues. He goes to a corner of the basement and hefts a plastic storage box. "With some staples. I was going to bring it to the truck, but I'm glad I left it down here."

He takes out a couple of blankets and tosses them around. We all wrap ourselves in them like we've been out in the arctic for hours. Huddled on the floor, I strain to hear anything, but it's gone eerily silent.

"What about the chickens?" Rose asks in a small voice, and no one says anything, because there isn't anything we can say.

Rose climbs onto my lap and Jack scoots close by, resting his head on my shoulder. I put one arm around Rose and the other around Jack, holding them close as I try not to imagine what is happening above us. Is our house buried in mud? Is everything we worked for ruined? And what if we can't get out of here? The thought is both terrifying and impossible to believe. *Our lives aren't that dramatic,* I think. *Things like this don't happen to us.*

Until they do.

For a while, no one says anything. We simply sit and wait, and the minute stretches into nearly an hour before Rose suddenly announces,

"I need to go to the bathroom."

"Oh, for heaven's *sake*," Bethany mutters while Jack asks practically,

"Number one or number two?"

"Number two," Rose admits, and Bethany groans.

"Okay," I say, and try to think of a solution. "Well, there's a bucket down here."

"I don't want to go in front of everybody," Rose cries, looking distressed and William interjects dryly,

"I think we've got bigger issues than having to watch you poop."

"You can go in the pantry," I tell Rose soothingly. "It's private in there."

"That's where we keep our *food*," Jack protests, and my voice rises in temper as I snap,

"Like William said, Jack, we've got bigger issues."

I take Rose into the pantry, closing the door and plunging us into pitch darkness as she squats miserably over a bucket.

"Mommy, I'm scared," she whispers, just as I hear an audible plop into the bucket and breathe in the accompanying stench.

"I am too, sweetheart," I tell her as I grope around for something for her to use as toilet paper and come up with a crumpled tissue from my cardigan pocket. "This is a scary situation. But we'll get through this."

"Will the chickens?"

"Chickens are smart, Rose. They'll hide in their coop."

"But the mud—"

In my mind's eye, I am picturing the relentless onslaught of mud sliding down the hillside, taking down whole trees. Truthfully, I don't think the chickens have much of a chance, but I don't want to think about that, never mind admit it to my seven-year-old daughter.

"All finished?" I ask instead, and she nods. I snap the lid onto the bucket and shove it into the corner of the pantry. Hopefully I won't forget to empty it at some point, when this is all over. Assuming, of course, I won't have far bigger issues to worry about, which I'm sure I will.

Back in the basement, everyone is still huddled in miserable silence. Josh hands out granola bars from his emergency stash, and we nibble them without much enthusiasm, even though no one has eaten this morning and we should all be hungry.

I feel too numb to process anything, my mind skating away from imagining upstairs. Our garden, our barns, our house, and of course the chickens. Is everything gone? And if it is, what do we now, assuming we aren't buried alive?

Despite my endless and annoying existential angst, I really don't want to leave Wildflower Valley. Even if we have to start over from scratch, I've *liked* this life. I've liked what we've built.

I just hope it isn't all gone.

After another miserable twenty minutes or so, William stretches, shrugging off his blanket, and goes to the bottom of the step. "I don't hear anything," he announces.

"Maybe that's because there's, like, twenty tons of mud above us so it's blocking all sound," Jack says. He sounds almost gleeful at the prospect; I don't think he's thought through all the implications.

"If there was that much mud," Bethany says, "the basement ceiling would have collapsed." She glances at Josh. "Right?"

"I'm afraid I don't know how much weight the ceiling could withstand," Josh admits. "But the prospect is making me wonder whether the basement was the best idea." He sighs, running a hand through his hair, and I can tell from the expression on his face that he's coming up against his ignorance and inexperience once more, and this time he's worried it might have far worse consequences than a broken tiller or a few blighted trees.

"I'm still going to check," William insists. "If I try the door, the worst that can happen is that it won't budge because there's a whole lot of mud covering it, right?"

"Right," I say, because that seems obvious, but… what if it's dangerous?

"I can go," Josh says, starting to stand, and William shakes his head.

"No, let me."

This is clearly a make-a-man-of-you moment, and so we let our fourteen-year-old son mount the basement stairs, having no idea what might happen next.

What happens is, William opens the door.

"It's fine," he calls down. "There's no mud anywhere. I don't think the house has been touched."

Which makes me feel equal parts relieved and stupid. Have we been crouching down in the basement for the better part of the morning for no good reason? Maybe the rest of the valley residents will be laughing at us, revealing our noob status once again, while they sit on their front porches and watch the show.

"The house is okay?" Josh asks. He sounds equal parts incredulous and disappointed, which I understand. Maybe we really have been stupid.

"Yes, but…" William's voice trails off as he walks through the house. In the gloom of the basement, we all stare at each other uneasily. Then, almost as one, we scramble to standing, shedding our blankets, and race upstairs, to see for ourselves.

The first sunburst of relief I feel at seeing our house is intact and mudless is tempered by a creeping dread at William's continued, ominous silence. When I see him standing in the mudroom, staring out back, I know we have not escaped unscathed.

Even so, I am not prepared for the devastation that has been wreaked upon our smallholding until I join William in the mudroom and stare out at what was once our backyard, vegetable patch, and orchard.

At first I can't even make sense of what I'm seeing. Where are our neat rows of new plants and the fence that surrounded them? The saplings in the orchard, tilting their young leaves to the sun? The neatly divided lines of our property, which had fallen into such pleasant places? All I see is churned-up mud, strewn with sticks and stones.

And then, with a hollow, numbing sensation, I realize just how much is gone. Our vegetable patch, the whole half-acre I thought was too much, save for one row of spinach, is completely covered by mud. All those new plants have been drowned in a sea of dirt.

The twelve tender saplings that made up our little orchard have disappeared under the onslaught, perhaps gone forever. Our chickens, thank the Lord, have survived, roosting on top of our chicken coop, clucking anxiously and ruffling their feathers, but the chicken run itself has been overcome, as has most of our yard.

The mud stopped just ten feet from our house, a sludge that even now continues to ooze ever onward.

I can barely believe it. All that hard work, that hope and toil, *gone* in an instant. I stay silent, because I have no words. No one else seems to, either, because we've all come to stand here, looking out at the view that I loved so much, and which now feels ruined—if not forever, then for a good long while.

How could this have happened?

While we're all still silent, we hear someone else approach.

"Coo-ee!" It's Hooch's standard call, as cheerful as ever, which is already enough to bring tears to my eyes.

"Hooch..." Bethany turns from the scene of devastation that

is our backyard and runs to the front door, throwing it open. "Hooch!" she calls, her voice filled with relief. "Are you okay?"

"Right as rain," comes the cheerful reply. "Although mebbe that's not the best comparison, just about now."

I laugh, the sound giddy and maybe even hysterical. I'm so glad to hear Hooch, but I'm still trying to make sense of what has happened to our lives.

"Maybe not, Hooch," I tell him as I walk toward the front door. "But it's certainly apt." I don't realize I'm wiping tears from my eyes until Hooch gives me a hug.

"Oh, Miss Abby," he says, sounding genuinely upset. "Y'all got hit?"

"Just the garden." I take a gulping breath. "It could have been so much worse."

Hooch nods seriously. "That it could have. I've just been down to the Hoffenbergers, and they ain't got nothing left."

I blink, even more shocked than I was before. "Wait... what?"

Hooch nods again, even more somber. "The mudslide took their whole place out. Everything's covered—the barns, the coop, the house. Good thing they decided to evacuate this morning, because otherwise, Lawd help us all, they'd have been buried alive."

Chapter Twenty-Two

I am walking away from the house, into the woods, my heart so very heavy. It's been four days since the mudslide, but it feels like an absolute epoch. It's as if my whole world has completely transformed in the space of a single week.

After the mudslide, we were numb with shock for a little while. It was just so hard to believe that so much of what we'd worked for was *gone*... our garden, our orchard... and what about the Hoffenbergers? That beautiful dream homestead I'd so admired and envied, wondered if we could one day have something similar...

According to Hooch, it was all under ten feet of mud, every last bit of it. Thank goodness Allie and Bill had evacuated, along with all their animals. There was no loss of life, just a terrible loss of dreams.

Hooch's place had, amazingly, escaped the mudslide completely. So had the Peppers, on the other side of the valley, and Miss Barbara, farther up. While I was glad for them, it didn't really make me feel any better. What would happen to the Hoffenbergers? And what about us?

In the ghost-like mist of a miserable morning, we went out to survey the damage on our own property. The rain had finally stopped, but everything was still dank and damp and gray, which certainly suited our somber mood. The chicken run, William insisted, could be repaired. The wire was twisted and bent, the posts had been knocked down by the onslaught of mud, but he said it could be fixed with some effort and elbow grease, and we chose to believe him.

The coop itself, along with the barns, had, somewhat amazingly, survived. Our young trees in the orchard were up to their necks in mud, but their tops stuck out valiantly; by the time the mud had reached our property, it seemed to have slowed enough not to utterly obliterate things, but rather just cover them up. Whether our little trees can handle that amount of mud remains to be seen. Hooch, who admittedly is no expert, declared it was fifty-fifty.

And then there's our beloved vegetable patch, our half-acre of tender young plants and seedlings just starting to take root, thrusting their pale green heads to the sky... all of it now under several feet of sludge. It's safe to say, I'm afraid, that our garden is gone. We can plant again for a later harvest, some things anyway, but the full harvest we were hoping for is no more.

I tell myself it could be worse, it could be *so* much worse, as it is for the Hoffenbergers, and even they escaped with their lives, sitting out the mudslide at a Residence Inn in Morgantown. We could have *died*, I remind myself, again and again. Some people did, not in Wildflower Valley, thank goodness, but in other places around the county where the rain was relentless, and the mud slid and slid.

I should be thankful, and I *am*, but there's an ache deep inside of me that I can't shift, of sorrow for the Hoffenbergers, whom I saw yesterday, both of them looking utterly shell-shocked, and for us, with no garden, no orchard, and a mountain of mud to clean up.

It's not the end of the world. It really isn't. But it still feels like the end of *something*. I just have to figure out what.

And so I walk through the woods, letting my palms skim along the rough bark of the trees, the ground damp and soft beneath my feet, the rich smell of earth and forest rising on the misty morning air.

I'm sad, but I'm also oddly, unexpectedly hopeful, maybe because this setback hasn't derailed me the way I once thought it would have. It's only made me more certain. We *can* recover from this. We can replant the orchard, the garden, rebuild the chicken run, whatever it takes. We can keep going, and we can thrive, because if we can survive this, we can survive anything.

Right?

A sigh escapes me, long and low and weary. Yesterday I held Allie in my arms and had no words, which was probably better than if I'd offered her some platitudes that wouldn't mean anything, and might even be insulting. But I felt as if she and Bill were shrinking before my very eyes, all they'd worked so hard for gone in an instant. How can that happen? How can the God the bluegrass band at church has been praising with such relentless cheer allow such a thing to happen?

It's an age-old question, I know, and a pretty shallow one. There are far worse tragedies and injustices to get upset about, and yet this is the one that hits home. This is the one that makes me want to shout *why*?

In the middle of the forest, I stand still. The sky has begun to clear, shreds of cloud evaporating into mist, and the trees tower all around me, with columns of sunlight streaming through the spaces between their trunks, looking tangible enough to touch. I rest my hand on the trunk of a tree and look up through the canopy of leaves to the sun high above, shining benevolently down like it never rained at all.

I blink, squint, and then stand on my tiptoes. Is that... I reach for a low-hanging branch and pull it down toward me, amazed. Why yes, yes, it is. It's a tiny, hard, nut-brown apple, just starting to grow. I can't believe it, an apple tree, right here in the middle of the impenetrable and kind of scary woods.

I let go of the branch and look around, and that's when I see more apple trees—at least half a dozen, an actual *orchard*, overgrown and forgotten, here in the forest. Was this someone's pride and joy once upon a time, fifty years ago or more? Perhaps the little orchard now covered in mud was once bigger, or perhaps there was a farmhouse that has fallen down and been forgotten by the generations that have come homesteaded here since. I might never know, but either way, this apple tree feels like both a gift and a blessing. A reminder.

Life goes on, both because of and despite our puny efforts, and it's important to remember that. To accept it. I pluck one tiny apple from the branch, curling my fingers around it, and then I head back home.

Josh has been struggling these last few days, although he hasn't admitted as much. He's been quiet, which is unusual for him, and even though the kids have been far more pragmatic than I ever expected them to be, and Rose has developed resilience in spades, helping to dig out the chicken run and leaving Bruce in her bed all day, thank *goodness*, Josh doesn't join in, at least not the way I once would have expected him to, no question.

He's kept himself apart, busying himself with various tasks—ditch-digging at the top of that list—but I feel a sense of disappointment and even depression emanating from him, and it worries me. I've always needed him to be the cheerful, optimistic one, but maybe that's not really fair.

Maybe it's my turn to be that person for him.

I find him in the barn, attempting to replace the broken tiller blade that we never fixed, since Hooch said the motor had probably given out, as well. I already sense it's going to be a futile task, but I understand the need to do *something*.

"Hey," I say softly, and he glances up briefly before continuing to work.

"Hey." His voice is quiet, guarded.

"I thought we'd consigned that to the dump," I remark carefully, trying for a light tone, but not *too* light.

"Well, we're going to need it again, once we get rid of the mud, and the Hoffenbergers can't lend us theirs anymore, so..." He shrugs, his gaze fixed on the broken tiller.

"Josh..." I hesitate, because this is kind of new territory for us. Josh is the one who jollies, who picks up the pieces, who keeps it all together. "Are you okay?" I ask gently. "Because these last few days you've seemed... a little down."

He lets out a huff of humorless laughter. "Well, considering we suffered a mudslide, lost our entire orchard and garden and *nearly* lost our house as well as our lives... I think I'm doing all right."

That's true enough, I suppose, but I still sense there's something else going on. Something deeper. "The mud stopped a good twenty feet from the house," I tell him. "It wasn't as close as all that."

"But it could have been." There's a tremor in his voice that both surprises me and makes me ache.

"Josh..." I take a step toward him. "You don't... you don't blame yourself, do you? For any of this? Because it was a natural disaster, and I'm pretty sure those are blame-free, by definition."

"Shouldn't I?" The words burst out of him. "I'm the one who came up with this crazy idea. I found this property and didn't check it through properly, not even the trees or the fact that it could flood, or a mudslide could happen." He draws a shaky breath. "And… if I hadn't been so gung-ho, would any of you come on board? Really?" He turns to look at me with pain-filled eyes. "I feel like such a stupid cliché. I'm the dad who's having a midlife crisis and drags his family along to some dangerous situation just to prove he's still a man."

"I think that's a movie, actually," I tell him in an attempt at levity. "Maybe *The Mosquito Coast*?"

A smile tugs at his mouth and then dies. "I'm serious, Abby."

"So am I," I say firmly. I am certain about this. "This is not your fault. And yes, you were gung-ho, but so were the kids. So am I. We all chose this, and you didn't drag us anywhere." I gaze at him steadily, willing him to believe me, because I absolutely mean it. "You told me there would be setbacks. We both knew that going in. Every homesteading YouTuber ever says the same thing. It's not an easy life, but it's a good one, and we all chose it."

Josh shakes his head. "What if something had happened to us? To one of the kids? What if we had been buried alive, like Bethany said?"

I shrug, manage a smile even though the image he paints is terrible. "But we weren't."

He sighs, casting his gaze to the ceiling. "I still don't know if going to the basement was the right call. Maybe it was yet another stupid move I've made since we came here. Maybe it could have killed us."

"Josh," I warn him, my tone turning stern, "this is starting to sound like self-pity." I wag a finger at him, gentling my words with a smile. "You made the best decision you could with the information you had. And we are going to make a *lot* of stupid moves, because we moved here without knowing that much, and we're learning on the job, as you've said yourself, many times. This is a setback, a big one, but it's not failure, and it's not irreversible."

He's silent, gazing down at the broken tiller, his shoulders bowed. "Maybe," he says at last, the words coming out on a gusty sigh, and I can't tell if I've started to convince him.

"Look." I hold out my hand, the little apple resting on my palm.

Josh squints at it. "Is that..."

"An apple. There are some apple trees up on the hillside, in the forest. There must have been an orchard there, once. Well..." I let out a little laugh. "There still is."

He takes the apple and examines it. "Amazing," he says quietly.

"I know, right? We still have an orchard. And..." I don't want to get *too* philosophical, but something about those apple trees moved me. "It's a reminder that this whole thing is bigger than us. That life is. And we can choose to be part of it, to keep going... but all this will be here a lot longer than whatever we manage to build will, mudslide or no." I gesture to the valley all around us. "And maybe that's a good thing."

He glances at me, his eyes crinkling at the corners in a way I know and love. "And despite your doubts, you still want to keep going?"

"My doubts were just me coming to accept my place in the world," I correct him with a smile. "And yes, absolutely, more than ever. I want to dig out our garden and plant again. Repair the chicken run and try to save our trees or, if we have to, buy more. And..." I pause. "I want to help the Hoffenbergers."

Josh's eyebrows lift. "How?"

"They want to stay in Wildflower Valley and rebuild..." I feel my way through the words, the idea that has been growing inside me. "But they'll need somewhere to stay."

Now his eyes widen, and understandably so. "With *us*?"

"Just for a little while," I say quickly. "They're hoping to build something small to start, to winter in. And our extra bedroom will be finished in a few weeks. Until it is, we can sleep in the attic, and they can have our bedroom."

Josh nods slowly, accepting, even though I still have my own doubts. "You've really thought this through."

"Well, sort of." I'm really still not convinced I will survive living with Allie for several weeks or even months, but I know that's what a good neighbor does, a Wildflower Valley one, and I want to do it. "What do you think?" I ask.

"I think…" Josh says slowly as he straightens. "It's a good as well as kind idea." He pulls me toward him, and I come gladly, grateful he's smiling. "Thank you," he says seriously. "For talking me down from the ledge."

"It felt more like talking you up from a pit," I quip. "I'm the one usually on the ledge."

"True enough." His arms tighten around me. "Still… I'm grateful. For you, and the kids. For being here, for being willing."

"We're here and we're doing this," I remind him, smiling.

And that's true whatever comes next, I tell myself. The future will always be uncertain, but at least, I remind myself, we're facing it together… Hoffenbergers included. Whatever comes next… we're here and we're doing this.

As I hug Josh and we head out into the sunshine, I realize I can hardly wait.

***

Join the Bryants in their next adventure, as the Hoffenbergers move in and they replant their garden in *Time to Grow*, available for pre-order now.

Enjoyed *Both Feet In*? There's more to discover! Find out about Kate's other books on her website https://katehewittbooks.com/

Dear Reader,

Thank you so much for reading *Both Feet In*, the second book in my Wildflower Valley series. I'm not a homesteader myself, although I have big dreams of growing vegetables and raising chickens just like the Bryants do. Any mistakes in homesteading wisdom are, I'm afraid, a sign of my own inexperience, although I have loved all the research and it has inspired my own homesteading adventures.

I have plenty more stories in store for the Bryants, so please do look up my other books on http://wildflower-valley.com, or my other books on my website http://www.katehewittbooks.com. You can also join my Facebook group, Kate's Reads, where I like to discuss books, TV, cooking and life with my readers.

For news on my books as well as giveaways and special offers, please join my newsletter which can be found on my website and keep a look out for more Wildflower Valley adventures!

Happy reading,

Kate

P.S. Turn the page to read the first chapter of *Time to Grow*, the third book in the series!

Time to Grow
Wildflower Valley Book 3

Chapter One

Sometimes life is easier when you just give up. Obviously, that's not a maxim I want to live by, *or* have as my epitaph, although it might be apt, all things considered. But when it comes to Allie Hoffenberger and me sharing a kitchen, well, I guess I've learned to pick my battles.

Let me recap: three months ago, my family and I moved from the manicured suburbs of Princeton, New Jersey to the wilds—comparatively, anyway—of Wildflower Valley, West Virginia, although at this point, over three months in, I should be able to call it a holler, the way real West Virginians do. For some reason, the word doesn't roll off my tongue. I don't like pepperoni rolls either, a West Virginia specialty—so maybe I'm doomed.

I'm kidding. Sort of. The point is, we moved here, and there has been a lot of adjusting and growing to do. Noobs that we are, we discovered that all the trees in our little orchard had fire blight, and on the first day of plowing my husband Josh broke our brand-new tiller. We've been living in a building site as we try to make our dream home, while simultaneously realizing—at least I have—that maybe such a thing doesn't exist, and more to the point, shouldn't. It would be fair to say that there have been a few existential crises along the way—I seem to specialize in those—but I think I've got them mostly resolved. For now, anyway. Who knows what tomorrow holds, because I've surrendered my kitchen to my bossy but well-meaning (mostly) neighbor, and surely that is deserving of an existential crisis of its own.

Three weeks ago, a mudslide devastated our fledgling, half-acre vegetable patch, orchard, and chicken run, although thankfully our chickens had the sense to clamber onto the roof of the coop, and in doing so all eight of them, including two pesky roosters, survived. Still, it was a blow—our hard work, at the early stages as it was—had been comprehensively wrecked. Seeing your tender tomato plants covered in eighteen inches of sludge is dispiriting, to say the least.

Far worse, though, was the fate of our neighbors, Allie and Bill Hoffenberger. Their gorgeous homestead—house, barns, greenhouse, vegetable garden, all worthy of at least a million subscribers on YouTube, not that they're social media types—had been completely destroyed. Hence my kindly-meant offer for them to live with us while they got back on their feet. Bill insisted he could build a log cabin for them to winter in in just a couple of weeks, and I had the naivete to believe him, but so far he's yet to put two logs on top of each other.

It's okay, though. I understand. It's hard to get back on your feet when you've been dealt a full-on body blow. So my response was to give Allie my kitchen. My brand-new kitchen that the contractors had just finished and the builders just fitted, once the rain had stopped and they could get up the mud-slide-in-the-making that was our front driveway. I admired the six-burner range, the big wooden island, the acres of counter space, the window seat overlooking the pond, and the nook big enough for a table that seats ten from afar while Allie took up residence.

I lasted all of six days before I caved. I was chopping onions for a lasagna while Allie hovered over my shoulder, murmuring under her breath. It was early June, just a little over week after the mudslide, and we were all still feeling tender, Allie especially, I think, not that she ever admitted as much. She was stoical, insisting they could build again, even better this time, but I saw for myself the wreck of all their work—a homestead worthy of a magazine covered in mud, and so I was more than willing to cut her some slack.

But then she told me the right way to chop onions, which I didn't even know was a thing. Apparently, if you don't cut the root off till the end, then you won't look like you're crying. Who knew? Not me.

I wasn't looking like I was crying, anyway—I've got eyes like iron and a heart of steel, to boot—but Allie gave me that helpful advice, anyway. This was after six days of *many* such gems of helpful advice, from how to do hospital corners on bed sheets to the right temperature for the laundry—and, for the record, I am not someone who has *ever* separated whites from colors—to Rose's bedtime, which was far too late. To be fair, it *was*, but Rose is my seven-year-old, not Allie's, and in any case Allie and her husband Bill are estranged from their daughter Emily, so who are they to give parenting advice?

Not that I'd ever say such a thing. I'm not a monster.

And so I gave up my kitchen with mostly good grace. I put my knife down, turned to face her with what was meant to be a friendly smile.

"Allie, would you like to chop the onions?" I asked, all solicitude.

Allie looked taken aback, caught between wanting to grab the knife out of my hand and suspecting it wasn't a serious question.

"I'm just trying to help," she said with a sniff, which was such an

Allie thing to do. She'd been just trying to help since we'd moved in.

"No, seriously," I said, determined to mean it. "You're so much more experienced than I am in so many ways. If you want to run the kitchen while you're here, I totally get it." I smiled to take any potential sting from my words. "And, honestly, I'd appreciate it. There's so much work to do, and I could really use your help in here. Obviously, I don't want you to do anything you don't want to, but if you'd like to take the lead... please do."

I may have said the last through slightly gritted teeth, because I'm basically a bad person. But I *wanted* to mean it, so does that count for something? I hope it does. I felt badly for Allie. It was just she was driving me a little crazy.

In any case, she agreed with alacrity. She took up the knife, chopped the onions her way, and made a lasagna my kids had to choke down because she included way more vegetables than they were used to. Who puts celery in lasagna? Not me, anyway.

But really, it's all good. That was two weeks ago, and we're still figuring it out, but we're getting there. Or so I whisper to myself in the shower, while rocking back and forth under the spray, because sharing your tiny house—enormous kitchen addition aside—with two veritable strangers, one who is extremely fussy, is not easy.

I knew it wouldn't be, and I tell myself I'm still glad we did, but there we are. That's the unvarnished, unpalatable truth. This is hard, and I'm making the best of it.

I guess you could probably say that about most things in life.

In any case, there are so many things that are going well. Ed Wilson, the husband of my friend Emmy and a state forester, lent us his backhoe so we could clear the sludge from our orchard and vegetable patch. My husband Josh and fifteen-year-old son William repaired the chicken run, and it looks like at least two of the trees in our orchard survived. Ten others didn't, but I'm determined to look on the bright side.

As for our half-acre vegetable patch that was meant to feed most of us all winter—well, that didn't fare so well. In fact, it didn't fare at all. Who knew, but a mud slide does not act as an extra helping of compost, especially when your plants are barely more than seedlings, poking their cautious green head through the damp earth. Every single fledgling got crushed by the onslaught, from my oldest daughter Bethany's nascent herb garden to the tomato and cucumber plants I'd nurtured from seed, as tender as a mother hen with her chicks, or what I *imagine* what a mother hen with her chicks might be like, because the truth is, I don't really know.

We bought eight three-week-old chicks back in April, but so far we haven't had any mother hens. We haven't even had any eggs, but apparently we've got to wait around six more weeks for that.

In case you haven't guessed, which I'm sure you have, we're new to all this. Homesteading, homeschooling, gardening, carpentry, animal husbandry, all of it. We're self-confessed greenhorns, and we jumped in feet first and we're still figuring it out.

But we'll get there. More and more I believe that, and especially now with the Hoffenbergers' help. I mean that genuinely; Allie really is helpful in the kitchen, and Bill has helped Josh rebuild the chicken run, plant the trees in the orchard, and, as a former building contractor, advised on our addition. Did I mention we have builders in every day? Well, we do. After they finished the kitchen—which isn't *quite* finished, with wire dangling from various holes in the ceiling and walls—they started on the bedrooms. After they've added two more and another bathroom to the side of the house, they'll bump out the living room and add a wide front porch, the kind with porch swings and rockers and hanging baskets. We'll have to add all those, obviously.

By the time all that happens, our seven-year-old Rose will probably have graduated from college, but at least Josh and I will enjoy it, sitting out on our front porch by ourselves.

All in all, this homesteading life is what we chose, and we're making the best of it. More than that, we're enjoying it. Mostly. As Josh said and I've repeated many times, we're here and we're doing this.

With the help of our neighbors—Hooch, a self-proclaimed redneck, the aforementioned Hoffenbergers, groovy Miss Barbara with the slightly questionable herb garden, and my good friend Emmy Wilson who has nearly twice as many children as I do—we're making this work.

Mostly, anyway, and you can't ask for more than that, right? Except maybe the right to be alone in my own kitchen. Isn't that, at her heart, what every woman wants?

Or maybe just this woman, with a husband, four kids, two neighbors and a needy dog to deal with, plus the aforementioned chickens and another twenty meat chickens on the way. Plus, my husband and children are talking about getting a milk cow and maybe even a goat—although what for, I don't know. I don't even like goat's milk.

But that's all to come, and, so I tell myself, I'll have my kitchen back eventually. Besides, as they say, you can't have everything.

About the author

Kate Hewitt is the author of many novels of both historical and contemporary fiction. Her novels have been called 'unputdownable' and 'the most emotional book I have ever read' by readers.

An American ex-pat for many years, she now lives in New Jersey with her husband, two of her five children (the others are scattered across the globe!), their two Golden Retrievers and a slightly persnickety cat. Join her newsletter to receive updates and giveaways, or be part of her Facebook groups to discuss all manner of books. Links can be found on her website: https://katehewittbooks.com/

Her latest releases are *All I Ever Wanted*, *Where the Dawn Finds Us*, the third in her dystopian series Lost Lake, and *Playing for Keeps in Starr's Fall*, the second standalone in her new heartwarming series inspired by the Gilmore Girls. There's something for everyone so do check them all out, and be in touch as Kate loves to hear from readers. You can discuss Kate's books as well as others on her private Facebook group, Kate's Reads or read her thoughts on Substack.

Printed in Great Britain
by Amazon